Corrupt SAVIOR

BOOK 2
WAGES *of* SIN
DUET

TARA LEIGH

Corrupt SAVIOR
TAKES PLACE AFTER
CRUEL *Sanctuary*

To truly enjoy Damon and
Aislinn's epic love story, you
should start at the beginning
with

CRUEL *Sanctuary.*

Tara Leigh
www.taraleighbooks.com
Cover Design: Regina Wamba, Mae I Design
Editing: Becca Hensley Mysoor, Edits in Blue
Karen McVino, Expressive Editing
Marla Esposito, Proofing Style
Formatting: Mesquite Business Services

Print ISBN: 978-1-7328010-7-3
eBook ISBN: 978-1-7328010-6-6

dedication

Becca, this one is definitely for you. Aislinn is Damon's bright light and while writing their story, you were mine.

acknowledgements

My readers—you are EVERYTHING!!! I love reading your reviews and value your honest feedback! And all those messages/posts/tweets/e-mails you send as you're reading—they make my day! **hugs** In so many cases you have become friends. Thank you for letting me into your lives!!

A huge thank-you to, Jessica Alvarez of BookEnds Literary Agency. Your critiques and career guidance are invaluable!

Becca Hensley Mysoor, I absolutely love our long phone calls. Your insight on story structure and plotting is invaluable. You are stuck with me forever!

Karen McVino, I love all your comments and voice messages! So thrilled to work on another story with you!

Marla Esposito, thank you for your attention to detail and taking my book baby on vacation with you!

Regina Wamba, thank you for this GORGEOUS cover! (and for putting up with me!)

Devyn Jensen, thank you for ALL THE THINGS!!! You are an expert at everything I don't know how to do and I am so grateful!

Danielle Rairigh, working with you is such a pleasure! Thank you for your feedback, encouragement, and friendship.

Yamina, you are the sweetest to always check up on me! Thank you for all of your feedback on this book and for all our messenger chats. You get my brand of crazy! ;)

Nadine, thank you for putting up with my never-ending screenshots and "So, is this better?" questions!! You are too good to me!!

Melissa Teo, I know you have a "real" job now but you are never getting rid of me. Thank you for your friendship, daily have-you-heard? messages, and so many gorgeous graphics and teasers!

Serena McDonald, I heard your voice in my ear as I was writing this book—I hope Damon is dirty enough! Thank you for encouraging me when I'm feeling lost and helping my books reach more readers. Your minion messages always make my day.

Amy Halter, you are one of the sweetest and most supportive women I know. I am so lucky to have you in my corner!

Lana Kart, getting your seal of approval was a career goal of mine—thank you so much for the multiple chances, lol! I was so nervous to reach out to you, but you couldn't have been nicer. And I love our ridiculously long voice message chains!

A.L. Jackson, thank you for sharing your fabulous daughter with me. You are an inspiration and a role model in this crazy, chaotic, wonderful business.

Nicole Westmoreland, thank you for your friendship and for helping me with the VIPs! I love all our message chats!

Maria Kusel, you make such pretty things for me. I love my banners and bags and bookmarks. And I love you, too!

Ava Harrison, what a small world! Beefalo BFFs 4eva!

Stephanie Sab, thank you for being my go-to for all things signings!!! I hope we can actually meet up at one of them soon!

Abby O'Shea & Christina Westrich, thank you so much for taking a chance on me. It is such an honor to be a part of The Romance Reveal Book Box, and I am truly grateful for the opportunity!

Julie Linhart, you are the queen of swag and make every order a pleasure!

Mary Dube, no matter where you are in social media land, I will follow you. Although ... my favorite place is in my messages. Love, you!

Angie McKeon, connecting with you over my Lies Duet was completely surreal, and you are every bit as sweet as your reviews. Thank you for taking a chance on me!

Lauren Layne and Anthony LeDonne of Last Word Designs, thank you for my gorgeous logo and website, **www.taraleighbooks.com**!

Lexi Smail, you taught me what great editing is. I miss you and the team at Forever Romance, and hope we will work together again one day!

S.L. Scott, you have become one of my very favorite people. I love our chats about book world business and nonsense, writing and kidlets!

Skye Warren, you are incredibly generous with your expertise and the 2018 Romance Author Mastermind conference was a career highlight. Thank you for everything you do for this industry.

Sierra Simone, I devour every word you write and come away inspired and refreshed. (after shaking my fists in the air and wishing for one thimbleful of your talent).

To my family & friends—I adore you all … and I'm sorry for ignoring your calls when I'm writing!

My neighbor Cindy, you are a wonderful friend to me and an absolute blessing to my kids. Moving next door to you was one of the smartest decisions Stephen and I ever made!

My Beta Beauties: Amy, Amy, Danielle, Lana, Nadine, Yamina—thank you for your insight and encouragement! Each of you helped breathe life into Damon and Aislinn, and they are so much better for it.

Thank you to all the amazing bloggers and author assistants who have become a virtual cheering section for me, and I hope that I do the same for you. You are the unsung heroes in this wonderful place called Romancelandia and I am so grateful for your support.

In particular, Andrea, Ashley, Astrid, Aurora, Brigid, Brittany, Carol, Cat, Chele, Christy, Elizabeth, Emma, Gemma, Jackie, Jaime, Jemima, Jen, Jenn, Jessica, Karen, Kelly, Liana, Lisa, Mary, Mariela, Marta, Megan, Meghan, Nikki, Paramita, Pernilla, Pavlina, Sara, Sarah, Sheila, Siobhan, Stephanie, Vanessa, Wendy, Weronika … and so many more. I can fill the pages of this book with everyone that has made me laugh and smile and cry with your incredible reviews and personal messages. I hope you enjoy this book—believe me when I tell you, you are the reason I spend endless hours at my laptop. I hope you enjoy this one!

My ARC Team, you remind me why I write. Thank you for your encouragement and honest feedback. Writing is a solitary endeavor, but because of you, it isn't a lonely one.

My Bookstagram Team, I am in awe of the creativity, energy, and effort you put into your bookstagrams! I hope you enjoy playing with this duet!

RWA and CTRWA, I wouldn't be published without my membership in these incredible organizations, and I've met some of my best author friends at meetings and conferences.

Grandma, you left me nearly twenty years ago, and not a day goes by that I don't miss you. For any smokers reading this—put the cigarette down. Think of the people in your life who will one day watch you struggle to breathe and when you lose that battle, will miss you desperately.

Thank you to my mom for never ripping all those "bodice-rippers" out of my hands as a teen/tween, and to my dad for showing me what it means to work hard. (Who needs weekends or vacations, anyway?)

Stephen, thank you for being a wonderful husband and supporting my dreams. I love you. Logan, Chloe, and Pierce, thank you for being such great kids & genuinely considerate of my writing time. I am blessed to be your mother. Our lives are enriched by our sweet rescue puppy, Pixie. The wonderful organization that brought Pixie into our lives is Goofy Foot Dog Rescue, and if you would like to welcome a dog into your family or donate to their organization, please visit their website:
www.goofyfootrescue.org

And if you would like to see more pictures of Pixie and get updates on new releases, sales, and behind-the-scenes snippets, please sign up for my newsletter at
http://bit.ly/TaraLeighNwsltr.

Corrupt
SAVIOR

chapter one

Damon

"We have a problem."

Normally, I would dismiss Finley's statement as false. I don't have problems.

I have solutions. Answers. Schemes.

However, the fact that she is in my bathroom before I've even wrapped a towel around my hips is proof that I do indeed have a problem.

And I know.

I know before I slick the water from my hair. I know before I glimpse the pained expression on Finley's face. I know before she utters a single detail.

Aislinn Granville is in trouble.

It's a problem, all right. A big fucking problem.

My problem.

Because Aislinn Granville is *mine*.

However, even as fury seethes within my bones, it is an altogether different emotion viciously attacking the rest of me. Fear.

Fear I won't ever lay eyes on Aislinn again.

Fear my mistake in judgment will be a fatal one.

Fear I never deserved her in the first place.

That the hell I'm now in is exactly where I belong.

That she's in a hell I cannot save her from.

It is fear that sends a cyclone of adrenaline whipping through my body. Ominous winds pummeling my ribs. Toxic rain corroding my skin, contaminating my veins and muscles and sinews.

But as that useless emotion works its way through me, it transforms into something else entirely. Rage. A rage so potent and powerful it becomes fuel.

"Where is she?" I ask, the initial spike of my heartbeat already slowing to a level that will allow me to operate with cold, hard, methodical logic. Aislinn's life may depend on it.

Finley responds as if she's reading from a report. "Final destination is currently unknown. She was abducted by a three-man team, one posing as a dog walker. The dogs attacked our men while she was pulled into a white van."

"A van?" Jesus Christ. A shard of composure breaks loose to stab at my brainstem. It is like the events of twenty years ago have come back to haunt Aislinn all over again. "Our men?"

But there is a difference between then and now. A big difference.

Me.

"Just puncture wounds from the bites, minimal bleeding. Once the van was out of sight, another van pulled up, someone whistled and the dogs released our men and jumped in. The first van drove a block and a half away before pulling into a commercial parking garage. It was abandoned there and I have a team going over it right now. The second van—"

"I don't give a fuck about the damn dogs," I snap. Maybe later, I will want the intel. But right now, all I care about is

Aislinn. "Security cameras in the parking garage?"

"I've already downloaded the feed, but the transfer of Aislinn from the van to another vehicle, a late model Jeep, was done out of range. I have a team analyzing it right now."

"Parking attendant?"

She shakes her head. "We found blood spatter in the booth, but no body. My guess is that they shot him and took the body with them."

Which means Aislinn might be lying in a pool of someone else's blood right now.

My gut is a painful, gnarled lump stewing in toxins. *When I find the fuckers who put her there, they'll be swimming in a red river of their own.*

"I'll be downstairs in a minute. All hands on deck, Finley. Getting Aislinn back, alive and unharmed, is all that matters."

She acknowledges my order with a quick nod and then spins on her heel.

Minutes later, I am in my basement lair, hair still damp, jaw unshaven. The hive of activity momentarily freezes at my arrival, everyone glancing away from what they were doing to regard me silently.

Christ. "Anyone not contributing to Aislinn's safe return is a participant in her abduction," I say loudly. "And don't think for a second I won't hold each and every one of you responsible. Get back to fucking work."

As pep talks go, it is less than impressive. But it is the truth, and every second counts.

Rather than heading directly into my office, I join Finley at her workstation. She is looking at me with one brow raised, a strange expression on her face. "What?" I snap.

Eyes that serve as a painful reminder of Aislinn's give a slow blink. "Remember who you are. Damon King doesn't lash out at his staff, and he doesn't—"

"Lose a woman he's sworn to protect?"

We glare at each other for a moment before turning our attention to the screens on the wall in front of us. But her point is taken. *Pull yourself together.*

Several screens contain images of a white van. Same for a battered blue jeep.

Neither would stand out on the streets of Manhattan.

There are closeups of two license plates, both New York. A man whose face is obscured by a Yankees ball cap walking a pack of German shepherds.

Aislinn tangled up in leashes.

Aislinn, her face upturned, mouth open as if saying something to the dog walker.

The dog walker, leashes gone, his hands wrapped around Aislinn.

Aislinn pulled through the open side door of the van.

Goddamn it. I work to swallow down the mangled knot of fury and shame taking up residence inside my throat.

I knew this would happen. I allowed myself to become emotionally invested in Aislinn Granville. To treat her as more than just a woman needing my protection. To care for her more than I should.

Who am I kidding? I've cared about Aislinn since I first saw her face on a picture scotch-taped to the cement wall of my prison cell.

But I had no idea that the woman herself would be even more enticing than her beautiful face and bombshell body.

No idea that her zest for life would reignite my own.

The one woman I shouldn't have has become the one woman I can't live without.

Consequently, I've made myself vulnerable to my enemies in a way I never have before.

I've put Aislinn in danger.

And I have no one to blame but myself.

I've treated Aislinn Granville like a prize to be won, a trophy to be claimed, the crown jewel of my empire.

But my empire is corrupt, and there are enemies at the gate.

Fuck that. My gate has been breached, my territory invaded.

My woman seized.

And now, I will go to war.

I stalk to my office, slamming the door behind me as I run frenzied hands through my hair and flatten my lips against the wounded roar threatening to explode from my throat. The cold mist that has climbed up my back and neck, inching beneath my hairline, isn't lingering dampness from my shower. It is itchy, clammy sweat that spreads across my skin as my gut twists and churns with a violent fury.

I haven't ever felt rage like this. Not even when I received the news of my mother's death while I was in prison. It was ruled accidental, but only because her murderer knew how to make it appear that way.

Act in haste, repent at leisure.

An expression my stepfather was particularly fond of. He said it often, like a tic. I may have hated the messenger, but the message itself is painfully true.

Back then, my carelessness and impulsivity resulted in a prison sentence, leaving my mother alone and vulnerable. I failed to protect the woman who had borne and raised me.

Her death was my fault.

Today, my capitulation and empathy have resulted in Aislinn walking straight into a trap. It was my responsibility to keep her from the cartel's clutches. And I failed. Miserably.

Aislinn's abduction is my fault.

My motherfucking fault.

I warded off previous attempts to take her. And yet, this

morning, I let her go.

Truth is a relentless bitch that eats away at my intestines. There is no avoiding it. No way to soften the blow. My Achille's heel has been severed with a rusty, jagged knife.

I allowed Aislinn to burrow beneath my skin, into the deepest, darkest crevices no one has ever seen. She brought light with her, and I'd basked in the unaccustomed warmth of her sun.

Because of that weakness, I allowed myself to be swayed by Aislinn's anger. By her misinterpretation of a ridiculous fucking text.

Most states have criminalized texting and driving now. Just a quick glance at words on a screen can distract from what's in front of you. And that momentary distraction can mean the difference between life and death.

We weren't in a car, but that's exactly just what happened. We were distracted by a fucking text.

The fact that I know who took her, and why she was taken, does not dilute my fury—or my fear—in the slightest.

Hugo Cruz ordered Aislinn's kidnapping, of that I have no doubt. But my most pressing concern is the Los Muertos soldiers responsible for executing his command. Have they touched her? Hurt her? Ra—

I grit my teeth against the word that explodes inside my brainstem, grinding the edges of my molars into dust. My heart is pounding, pumping blood and oxygen and outrage to every extremity. I can feel my muscles inflating, my veins expanding.

Hugo Cruz is a formidable enemy, with money and planning on his side.

What happened this morning happened *fast*. Twenty-seven seconds between Aislinn getting tangled up in the leashes to the arrival of the second van. It went unreported to the police, any pedestrians too distracted by the dogs to notice that Aislinn was being shoved into a van.

It was a well-planned, flawlessly executed attack.

Too well-planned to be a New York gang. Not bloody enough to be Russian or Korean.

Classic Los Muertos, through and through. Kidnappings are one of their favorite methods, and although they don't often operate on American soil, when they do, they are masters at avoiding police attention.

Cruz may have beaten me on the battlefield, but in the war for Aislinn Granville, I will not lose. I will take back what's mine.

And they will pay.

The monster Aislinn tamed has been brought back to life, resurrected by the vengeance flooding my veins. I am the man I was before her—the devil of New York City.

A savage with no soul, no conscience. Just an overwhelming hunger for blood, an unquenchable thirst for revenge.

I will have both.

And I will have Aislinn too.

Because I cannot live without her.

chapter two

Aislinn

I've had headaches before. Who hasn't? Hangover headaches. Hormonal headaches. Stress headaches. Too-much-junk-food-not-enough-water headaches.

This isn't a headache. This is … I don't know what this is. My brain feels like it is being crushed by my skull—a skull that has suddenly grown teeth. Big, sharp, ravenous teeth.

It is only as I am trying to figure out how to devour a bottle of Excedrin without moving, swallowing, or opening my eyes that I realize my head is the least of my problems.

Snippets of memory come at me in blurry patches. Damon's phone. The texts from Chad. Confronting Damon. Demanding to leave.

Then, stepping outside into the crisp morning air. Damon's driver standing beside an open door. His confused expression when I stop in the middle of the sidewalk. Getting tangled up with a dog walker. A sharp pain in my side. Hands at my waist. The white van.

The white van.

I force my eyes open, intending to study my surroundings.

I'm almost certain I'm not in the van anymore, and I'm definitely not moving.

My eyelids flutter … but nothing changes. I'm still in the dark.

A thick oppressive darkness I cannot blink away.

No matter how hard I try.

I press my lips together, keeping the high-pitched whine gathering in the back of my throat from escaping, whipping my head this way and that, looking for something, anything.

To my left, almost behind me, I see it. The spill of light beneath a door.

Am I … Am I in in a closet?

Not again not again not again.

Vertigo slams into me, the dizziness scrambling my brain. I focus on that faint amber slice bisecting the darkness, using it as an anchor to pull me back from the brink of hysteria.

I can't lose focus.

I'm not a little girl anymore.

I'm not collateral damage.

This time, I was taken alone.

This time, I am the target.

I was stolen from under King's nose. They want me.

According to Damon, New York is crucial to the cartel's lucrative drug empire. There are millions of dollars at stake. They want my father, the Manhattan DA, to hand over the keys to his city.

And I am the leverage Los Muertos needs to get my father to do their bidding. There are millions of dollars at stake.

I am valuable. Their bargaining chip. Their damn prize.

As the buzzing in my ears fades, I hear voices. Three men, I think. They are speaking a guttural Spanish that is a distant cousin to the language I understand, their dialect littered with rough-hewn consonants and deep-throated vowels.

No. I'm wrong. There's a fourth man. He's speaking

Spanish, too—but the accent and dialect are completely off. His words are choppy and curt, with no elongated r's or soft t's. He sounds … American.

The man in the baseball cap—the dog walker. I only vaguely remember his face now, but I am absolutely certain there was no spark of familiarity at first glance. A white guy with brown hair beneath his cap and, I think, brown eyes. The slightest hint of a five-o'clock shadow dusting his jawline. He wore jeans and a fleece zip-up.

He was a stranger.

Except, he was the same stranger I'd seen several times walking those same dogs.

A puzzle piece locks into place with an almost audible *snap.*

The dogs. The man. He was just waiting for the perfect opportunity.

And I gave it to him.

Stupidly, naively, foolishly.

My stomach clenches, bile rising up my throat. My mouth isn't covered, but I force myself to swallow it down.

I am living my worst nightmare. My most terrifying dream. Even more so because it was once real.

Now it's real again.

And worse. So much worse.

The terror coursing through my veins is more potent now. Because there is something else to fear. Not just that I've been taken. Not just that I was tossed, once again, into a white van.

What if I never return to the man I've been taken from? The man who has become my world. My heart. My everything.

Damon King.

I repeat his name silently in my mind, latching onto each syllable like a ladder that will take me away. Far, far away from here. Back to Damon himself.

If genies are real, if fairy godmothers exist, if there really is an angel perched on my shoulder—I would only ask for one thing.

To return to my king.

Ironic, since leaving him—running away from him—is why I'm in this situation.

I am consumed with an ache that supersedes the effects of whatever drug was injected into my bloodstream. This overwhelming torment isn't chemical. It's biological, welling up from the deepest parts of me.

Damon, I miss you.

For a moment, I allow myself to wallow in my own personal pity party. To gag on hopelessness. Choke on helplessness.

It is so awful, so thoroughly miserable, it almost— *almost*—feels good.

My mind drifts back to Damon himself. What is he thinking right now? How is he feeling?

Does he even know the meaning of the word, helpless?

I highly doubt it.

My dark knight is probably enraged right now. Probably plotting and planning and gearing up for an all-out war.

Like a balloon snagged by a sharp branch, those stifling emotions inside me break free. No way will I become some soft-spined, weak-willed damsel in distress, hoping and wallowing and waiting for my dark knight to rescue me.

To hell with that. I'm going to rescue my own damn self.

My heart is a hummingbird trapped within the curved cage of my ribs. Bones that are compressing my lungs, each breath delivering barely enough oxygen to keep from passing out.

I can't pass out again. I have to think. I have to figure out how the hell I'm getting out of here.

But it's as if a net woven of fear and confusion and panic has been thrown over my head. The more I try to escape its tattered confines, the more tightly I'm trapped.

Shit. Shit, shit, shit.

I give into it. I can't do anything else. Like back in my college days when I would drink too much and get the spins. Instead of feeling sick, I would close my eyes and pretend I was on a roller coaster. I would ride the ride until it passed.

So that's what I do. My skin tingles, my chest aches, my eyelashes are as heavy as bricks. There is a ringing in my ears, a scratchiness at the back of my throat, and my left side throbs from landing hard on the floor of the van. I catalog each ache and pain and uncomfortable sensation, an exhaustive list of ailments from the tips of my toes to the top of my head.

With each line item, the tightness in my chest loosens a bit, the blood in my veins becoming more of a fast moving current than a tsunami battering my organs.

I make my list. I check it twice.

And then I am able to breathe again, to think again, to finally move beyond my panic attack.

There are important issues to be addressed. A stream of fire ants that march inside my brain, each of them carrying a question on its back.

I already know who to blame. Hugo Cruz. He finally got his way, and the men who took me are his foot soldiers. Cruz himself is probably somewhere in Mexico, already using me as leverage against my father.

But now, here, I am being eaten alive by my need to know where I am and how I can escape.

Am I in Mexico, too?

I have no idea how long I was unconscious. But I'm not in the van anymore. Or in a car, train, or plane. I am sitting in a chair. I tentatively attempt to move my legs, but I can't.

My ankles are bound.

I move my wrists. They aren't bound but … I am bound to the chair itself. Almost as if someone took a roll of duct tape and used it to encircle my entire torso.

I study what little I can see. The floor is dark and smooth. Not evenly set like freshly poured cement or textured slabs like tile. Whatever it is, there is a thick layer of packed dirt over it. And the smell is … fetid and ripe. Like a centuries-old cellar.

How much longer before my captors realize I'm no longer unconscious?

They are playing a game of cards. Every instinct in my body is telling me to throw my head back and scream bloody murder. But I know that would be the wrong move. A potentially deadly mistake. Because I've been in this position before. I've been the captive of a madman.

I need to play it smart, pretend that I'm not even here.

Maybe they'll forget about me.

A nearly hysterical laugh begins to percolate inside my throat. Fat chance.

Two weeks ago, I would have scoffed at the idea of one of my father's enemies resorting to kidnapping. Every Manhattan DA has enemies, especially when they are gearing up for a mayoral campaign, and James Granville is no exception. My father's enemies run attack ads, donate money to political opponents, dig up dirt on affairs, and hint at tax evasion.

They do not, however, drug and kidnap women off the streets of New York City.

But my father is a corrupt politician who has made an enemy of one of the most powerful cartels in the world.

Los Muertos isn't playing politics.

They aren't playing at all.

And I'm certainly not laughing.

They've attempted to kidnap me twice already.

Apparently, the third time is the charm.

I was so thoughtless, so careless. So stupid.

Walking away from Damon because of something I saw on his phone. Words he didn't even write.

If I had just talked to him, fought with him, I wouldn't be here right now.

Damon. There is a deep twist and pull inside my belly as I think about him again. A yearning.

As if a piece of me is missing right now. Him.

I was hurt and confused when I confronted Damon in his bedroom. I left because I needed space, some distance to think clearly, objectively.

Well, now I have it. How much space, I don't know.

Twenty years ago, I discovered my storybook perfect life wasn't a fairy tale. That not every man is someone's Prince Charming.

Damon isn't like any prince I've seen inside the pages of a book.

He is a dark king. An arrogant dictator. And as he enjoys reminding me, a skilled lover.

He is all of these things.

And maybe he is trying to save me.

Maybe.

But this political princess is no damsel in distress.

I got myself into this mess and I'll save my damned self too.

chapter three

Aislinn

I can't take my eyes off the images of Aislinn. Especially one in particular.

The one where the damn leashes have trapped her like a firefly in a spider's web. She looks almost … amused. Her mouth is slightly open, the corners just beginning to pull up into a smile. Looking at the dog walker who clearly isn't a dog walker at all, probably about to strike up a conversation, or offer an apology even though she's not at fault.

But that's who Aislinn is. An unpredictable spitfire. A woman who thinks the best of people, despite having seen the very worst in them.

She thought the best of me.

Even after I warned her not to.

Even after I told her exactly who I am.

The filthiest motherfucker you'll ever meet.

Aislinn saw light in my darkness and called it beautiful.

I should have told her it was just her own reflection.

Before she became mired in my filth. Before I trapped her with my own leash.

And, after all that, I couldn't even keep her safe.

King, you said I wasn't a prisoner here. Either I am, or I'm not.

Those were Aislinn's last words to me. My spitfire burned so brightly, I'd been blinded by her. And because I didn't want to dim her flame, I let her go.

Let her walk right into a trap.

And now, her flame might just be extinguished forever.

I can't let that happen. I won't.

The images my security cameras had captured—images of Aislinn, of the last moments she was mine—play in a relentless loop on my wall.

Echoing inside my mind.

Black stilettos stabbing at the pavement. Black skirt concealing and revealing in equal measure.

Blonde mane falling in an undulating ripple down her back.

The anger and frustration that filled her chest during our confrontation leaking out in the crisp Manhattan air. Maybe even disappearing entirely, like a burst balloon, when she found herself entangled on the sidewalk.

Do you like dogs, Aislinn?

I don't even know the answer to that question.

I thought I knew all I needed to know about Aislinn Granville.

Basic facts. Data.

Age. Date of birth. Height, weight, eye color.

The look of flushed annoyance on her face when I said something she didn't want to hear. The imperious attitude she wore on her back like a mantle of porcupine spikes. The muffled sound of her scream when my head was buried between her thighs.

But I don't know the small, simple things like whether Aislinn prefers dogs or cats or fucking iguanas. Pools or beaches. Morning hikes or evening strolls.

I want to know, damn it. I want to know everything about her.

Most of all, where she is right fucking now.

Something about the images bothers me. Something I can't quite pinpoint. I pace my office looking for something—anything—that doesn't fit.

And then finally, I see it, like an exclamation point.

"Finley!"

I'm too impatient to wait for her to walk into my office. Instead, I'm out my door and into the larger main space. Like before, my team stops what they are doing to give me their focus. But this time I don't mind.

I point at one of the images. "There. The guy should have both hands open when he grabs her. But he doesn't. One hand is closed like he has something in it."

Finley's eyes widen in understanding as she taps a button on her headset. "I want the area swept for whatever our guy might have been carrying. Something he may have dropped. Possibly a syringe."

Syringe.

I swallow at the word, but it makes sense.

Because the one image of Aislinn I'd been avoiding, the one image that didn't make sense, was the very last one my cameras had captured.

Pulled backward through the open door of the van, there is no struggle on Aislinn's face. She looks relaxed, even content. As if what's happening isn't a surprise.

She looks as if she hadn't put up a fight.

And damn it, if there is one thing I know about Aislinn Granville—my spitfire—she is a fighter.

To Juliana, the analyst standing beside her, Finley adds, "I want you digging through Los Muertos communications harder than ever. I don't care if a message appears to be innocuous conversation between a kid here and their sick grandparent in Mexico—I want it triple checked."

Juliana nods and spares me only a flickering glance before rushing off.

"And you," Finley motions toward another of our analysts, "get outside and walk the block like a tourist. Take pictures, look in windows, study the trash on the sidewalk. If there's anything unusual, I want to know it."

As the analyst jogs to the elevator, I run unsteady hands over my face. "I need her back." The words crawl up my throat, caught somewhere between a rasp and a growl. It is a statement of fact. Undisputable.

Finley's jaw is tense as she nods, her gaze intent on the screens covering the wall in front of us. "I know.

chapter four

Aislinn

You're a fucking cheat.

You can't play for shit. I don't need to cheat to take your money.

Why are we playing cards? I say we play with that girl—

Not yet.

How much longer do we have to wait? I can smell her pussy from here.

She can't scream if my dick is in her mouth.

I listen to their disgusting banter through the closed door. Three assholes who want to rape me. One who argues that they can't … yet.

Hugo Cruz must have told them not to.

But if they dare to try, they are going to have one hell of a fight on their hands. The first one who stuffs his dick in my mouth will have it bitten off.

For now, I remain quiet, keeping the screams bottled up inside my throat. Locking my questions and pleas behind gritted teeth and the tight seam of my mouth.

I stay still, despite muscles that scream from inactivity, from tension, from my purposeful paralysis.

The only movement I allow myself is the steady twitch of my fingers. My nails dig crescent moon shapes into my palms until I'm sure I've broken skin. It is a release, the only one I can afford.

Time passes. I have no way of knowing how much, although my bladder tells me that it's been long enough.

But I remain quiet. I remain still.

And I listen. Another game is dealt, more complaints about playing cards when they could be raping me. Much of their conversation is unintelligible. But there is one phrase I hear over and over.

El rey corrupto.

The corrupt king.

They could be talking about Damon.

Or … anyone else they consider corrupt. Like a powerful politician.

My headache is getting worse.

Every thought of Damon is a liberal pour of salt on an open, festering wound. He must be going crazy right now. And the thought of him hurting … it's almost unbearable.

He's blaming himself right now, I'm sure of it. That little boy who wanted to save the world is still inside of him. The little boy who lost everyone who ever cared for him—his grandparents, his mother. The little boy who became a vengeful beast of a man. A man I l—

The ring of a phone draws my attention, silencing both the crude banter and the noise inside my own head.

There is a mumbled "hello." An emphatic "yes" repeated several times in quick succession.

And then, footsteps. *Shit.*

I squeeze my eyes closed at the sudden brightness that accompanies the squeak of the door hinge. But at the soft *click* that ricochets inside my eardrums—the unmistakable sound of a switchblade—I open them, blinking rapidly in an effort to clear my vision.

The man I recognize as the one walking those German shepherds in front of Damon's apartment, the one who took me, chuckles at the naked expression of fear that must be on my face. He inclines his head down toward my ear, his breath a humid, black licorice-scented gust that turns my stomach. "I should run this knife across your throat."

I have a sudden memory of my last night with Damon, when he pressed his own blade against my neck. I had been scared of the knife, but not of Damon.

Right now, the opposite is true. The blade is not all that impressive, but the man wielding it exudes resentment and agitation. Unpredictability.

"Let me go." It is the faintest of whispers as I dare a glance into his eyes.

They are a muddy brown, betraying no emotion. The knife presses harder. "You think I'll listen to you?"

"You're taunting the devil by keeping me here." Instinct won't allow me to swallow. The slightest movement could result in bloodshed. My blood. "Letting me go is the smart move. The only move."

I expect to feel a warm trickle on my skin any second.

I hold my breath, tension turning my limbs into marble.

There is a moment of stillness, a beat where time is so heavy, so expectant, it can't move forward.

The spell is broken with a flick of the knife. Not against my neck, but a sharp downward slice that rips through the tape binding me to the chair. I feel the tip nick the skin between my breasts, and when I look, there is a red line between them. A shallow cut that stings more than it bleeds.

Two more slices at my wrists and they are free.

But not for long. He grabs them in his hands and turns them over, unrolling my tightly clenched fists and dragging his thumbs over the self-inflicted marks I've left on the fleshy part of my palms. One eyebrow tics upward as he stares at the bruises on my wrists. "These are not from me." He glances down at my ankles. "You like it rough, huh?"

Regarding me with a knowing smirk, he drops my hands to thread his fingers through my hair, leaning down to leer into my face as he gives a sharp yank. "Maybe I should let Cruz's men have a taste of you."

Tears prick my eyes at the sting but I blink them back. I am both burning up with anger and frozen in fear. My teeth rattle from the strident dichotomy. "They'll regret it."

His smile widens as he releases my hair. "I don't think so." A chill races down my spine, coldness seeping into the surrounding tissue.

"The worst is yet to come for you, Granville. I'll make sure of it," he says, pushing a newspaper against my chest. "Now hold that and smile pretty for the camera."

I glare at his face as he takes a picture with his cell phone. But when he whistles to the men he was sitting with and a roll of duct tape comes flying his way, I force myself to adopt a more respectful expression. "I have to go to the bathroom."

"Not my problem."

"Please. I-I really can't hold it anymore."

He releases an irate sigh and kneels down, running the sharp edge of his knife along my inner thigh and from the bend of my knee to my calf. "Don't make me regret this," he warns.

Right now, it's all I can do to keep from peeing in my chair. "I won't," I lie.

The last fiber of tape is barely cut when my right knee comes up, aiming for the center of his face. It's stupid, I know. I don't have a plan yet, and no clear escape route. But I've maintained a passive facade for too long. I can't do it anymore.

Either his reflexes are faster than I expected, or my muscles are still weak from the drugs lingering in my system. I don't make contact and his fingers merely dig into my thigh as he grunts. "Nice try."

Not long ago, I'd heard Damon snap a man's neck in two and been concerned by his casual approach to violence. Today, given half a chance, I would do the same thing.

chapter five

Damon

I am not a patient man, and today is no exception. There is a storm raging inside of me. A violent, malevolent churning I've never experienced before, not even when I was faced with my mother's bruised, battered body. Not even when I was sentenced to years in prison. Not even as I sat behind bars on the day of my mother's funeral.

I should have heard from Cruz by now. Or Granville.

Or fucking Lytton.

My brain shifts into overdrive as I dart out of my office, checking in with Finley briefly before heading, not for the elevator bank, but deeper into the subterranean network of underground tunnels I know so well.

The quick pace of my footsteps echoes on cement as I walk a familiar route, breathing in the damp, musty smell so different than exists aboveground. I don't own every building above me, but the Manhattan underground tunnels have always held a particular fascination for me.

There is something appealing about thriving beneath the city's grid, traveling a path few know about.

Not today, of course. There is nothing appealing about this day—except the thought of getting Aislinn back.

And vengeance.

Bringing Aislinn down here was never a consideration. Her place is in the spotlight. She deserves sunshine and fresh air and the wind on her gorgeous fucking face.

I emerge at street level, several blocks away from the apartment building I live in, plowing through the crowded streets like an NFL running back. Shoulders hunched, weight slightly forward, eyes straight ahead.

The hostess standing behind the reception desk of the trendy midtown steakhouse cracks a wide smile as she steps out from behind it, angling one leg out to show off the swath of naked flesh between the hem of her miniskirt and the top of her knee-high black suede boots.

"Can I help you, sir?" She lowers her lids, showing off dark makeup evidently applied with a trowel, looking up through fake eyelashes that wave at me like spider legs.

I barely spare her a second glance. Frankly, the first one was more than enough.

I lunge through the door behind her, her heels click-clacking after me. "Sir!"

Heads turn in my direction as I walk swiftly through the restaurant. I am being less than discreet and haven't a single fuck to give.

I don't knock on the door that encloses the private dining room. I fling it open and stand there, bitterness traveling up my throat and infecting the air around me. "Lytton, a word."

He wipes his mouth with a napkin, looking distinctly uncomfortable as he addresses the others at the table. "As you can see, under James Granville, the office of the Manhattan DA has built relationships with citizens from all walks of our city." He stands. "Excuse me, I'll just be a moment."

Once he's edged around the corner of the table, I pivot on my heel and walk toward the back of the restaurant. The kitchen staff knows better than to protest as I stomp through their workspace, followed by Lytton. Exiting into the back alley, the door hasn't even closed before I have his lapels bunched within my fists.

Lytton's head makes a satisfying thud as I slam him up against the brick wall. "She's fucking gone."

He appears dazed, so I give him a shake. "Did you hear me? Aislinn's gone."

He blinks at me a few times before batting my hands away. I let him because I want answers more than the pleasure of making him squeal. "What do you mean, she's gone?"

"She's been taken."

His slack expression finally hardens into understanding. "Are you sure Aislinn didn't just get sick of your overly aggressive tendencies? I—"

"Shut the fuck up before my overly aggressive tendencies throw you in a fucking dumpster." My hands tighten into fists at my side. "My security feed picked up the entire thing. It happened this morning, in front of my apartment."

"Someone took her … on your goddamn doorstep?" His mouth gapes open. "The big, bad bully of New York City couldn't keep Aislinn safe? That sounds like a *you* problem, if you ask me."

I don't know what's pissing me off more—that Lytton doesn't realize he's partly to blame for Aislinn being in danger or that he's not at all worried about her safety.

Or his dig at my inability to keep her safe.

"Actually," I step back toward this pompous imbecile I'm forced to deal with, getting right in his face, "it's a *you* problem, because if anything happens to Aislinn, I'm going to rip your goddamn balls off and shove them down your scrawny little neck."

"We told you we weren't backing down. This is your fault. Not mine. And how do you know for sure it's Los Muertos? You've made plenty of enemies in this town, in case you're unaware."

My gaze narrows. I am not unaware. My list of enemies is long. It's the nature of my business. I deal in corruption and currency. Crime and cash. I will shoulder my share of the blame, but I will not allow Lytton and Granville to be absolved of their burden.

Lytton straightens his jacket. "Either way, for someone who talks a big game about controlling New York's criminal element, you are the biggest criminal of all. You ever stop to think you might just be hurting the city you claim to protect?"

"Not for a second," I shoot back.

"Fine," he says with a sigh. "What do you want from me?"

"I want a fucking moratorium on all high-level investigations into Los Muertos."

His eyes fly open. "Are you wearing a wire? Have the Feds—"

Now it's my turn to be shocked as I interrupt his bullshit. "Shut the fuck up. The Feds? Jesus Christ."

"Well, you're being particularly chatty today. For the record, I have made no unlawful agreements with you or anyone else. I assist the District Attorney with his agenda, and as such—"

Unable to help myself, I punch Lytton in the softest part of his gut. Not hard enough to do permanent damage or cause internal bleeding. Just enough to have him double over, gasping for air.

I bend down, close to his ear. "I need you to remember this feeling. The fear that grows stronger with each passing second your brain is deprived of oxygen. The panic that clutches at your throat when no air gets through. And I want you to remember that I can take away your ability to breathe, permanently." I pat Lytton's shoulder. "Can you do that for me?"

He offers a frantic nod, holding onto his knees.

"Good. Now, we both know what you've done. Just as we both know what I've done."

He sputters a cough and meets my eyes, managing to wheeze a barely audible, "Yeah, I do," before coughing again.

"The only thing that matters right now is getting Aislinn back, understood?"

"Understood. So long as you understand—" more coughing. "Understand that I know *everything*, King. Especially where the bodies are buried."

"You want to be one of them?" Lytton pales beneath his flush. "Then stop pissing on people willing to slit Aislinn's throat just to send you and Granville a message."

He staggers back to his feet, finally able to pull air into his lungs. "Your problems are much bigger than you think they are."

The ominous rasp sends a disquieting ripple across my nerves. "What the fuck does that mean?"

Lytton's features tighten, leaving me unable to discern whether he was issuing a legitimate warning or a meaningless rebuttal. "Forget it. Like I said, I have made no unlawful agreements with you or anyone else. I assist—"

I turn away from Lytton with a furious growl. "Get out of here."

He wastes no time opening the aluminum door and scurrying inside. But he doesn't close it. Instead, he stands just inside the building. A fresh gust of garlic and roasting meat hit me in the face. My stomach turns. "So, do I need to tell Granville that you've lost his daughter, or is this something you can resolve in the next few hours?"

On second thought, I should have killed him when I had the chance.

The wave of incredulous fury that swells inside my chest must make an appearance on my face, too, because Lytton lets go of the door. It closes before I can reach through it and grab him by the throat.

I'm calming myself down by plotting Lytton's murder when the door opens again and a phone comes sailing at my face for the second time today. I catch it midair to find Aislinn's face filling the screen, holding today's paper beneath her chin.

"This came just now?" I ask without tearing my eyes away from Aislinn's imperious stare.

The ice princess I first met, her sapphire blue eyes gleaming with a cold, calculating fury.

Thank God.

"Yes."

I send it to myself and Finley immediately, then slip the phone into my pocket.

"Hey, give it back."

I step inside, standing toe to toe with Lytton. "You'll get it back. Just as soon as I get Aislinn back."

chapter six

Aislinn

"Are we—" I clear my throat. "Are we in Mexico?"

I've waited to ask the question until we are halfway up the narrow set of creaky stairs. Until there is some distance between me and the three other men still sitting around a card table, the sharp edges of their malevolently appraising eyes chafing my skin.

The dog walker pauses to unlock the door at the top of the stairs, grunting when the key stubbornly refuses to turn. I have no idea where I am being led, but I don't want to go back downstairs. Surely, wherever he is taking me will be better, or at least offer the possibility of escape. The key finally turns, and dim sunlight hits me in the face.

Run.

A vice clamps over my arm. "Don't even think about it."

But it's all I can think about. Running. Escaping.

Living.

I throw my head back, this time making contact with his nose. His howl of outrage ends in a grunt when my elbow jabs into his ribs. I bolt forward, lunging up the last step and looking for a door or a weapon. A way to escape or a way to kill. Either would be an acceptable option.

I don't bother worrying about where I will go. Who I am running to. That doesn't matter, not right now. All I know is that I have a chance at escape, at freedom—and I'm taking it.

The pressure from my elbow, or maybe just the fact that I dared to use it, catches him off guard. He lets go of my arm to grab for the banister attached to the side wall, stumbling down a few steps.

I bolt, automatically looking for a door, a window, something leading outside, away from here.

The details of my surroundings barely register as I see exactly what I'm looking for and sprint in its direction. A door. My fingertips graze the rusted, wrought iron handle for a fleeting second before I am tackled from behind. My head slams against the ground. Hard.

My vision blurs, tears stinging my eyes.

"Fucking bitch." His insult is a guttural snarl, his mouth so close to my face a spray of spittle lands on my skin. "I should let Cruz's men rape you."

He hauls me to my feet, nearly dislocating my shoulder. I wince at the pain even as my eyes bounce around the space, looking for clues.

Although they only make me more confused. I'm in a church. An abandoned church. The space is long and rectangular, the small windows so dirty that, while sunlight gets in, it's impossible to see out. It is obvious that no one has worshipped here in a long time, if ever. Broken sculptures line the walls three-deep, a thick layer of dust covers the floor, and cobwebs cling to narrow, arched windows like tattered lace curtains.

"Where are we?" I ask, my head swiveling from side to side. I don't hear any traffic, no signs that we're still in

Manhattan.

"What difference does it make? A place no one can hear you scream—that's all you need to know."

I hold my head high, mustering my haughtiest glower and deciding to push my luck a little further. "You're not in charge. That photo you took, it's for Hugo Cruz, isn't it?"

The hand holding my arm tightens, the vein at his jaw bulging.

But we both know that I'm right.

"I wonder what he would do to you if he finds out that I've been hurt. To Cruz, I'll bet your life is worth a hell of a lot less than mine."

He practically flings me toward a tiny bathroom at the back off the chapel. It is obviously a newer addition, although it looks to be at least thirty years old. And filthy.

If the door worked, I would have slammed it in his face. But it hangs crookedly by just one hinge, swinging awkwardly when I attempt to close it. "Would you mind turning around?"

His roar of laughter is answer enough, but he adds, "Forget it," anyway.

I lift my torn skirt and hover over the seat, lowering my gaze to the cracked tile beneath my feet and wincing in shame as the sound of my urine hitting the bowl echoes against the walls.

Privacy is a luxury.

I remember King's words as I flush the toilet and unsuccessfully attempt to squeeze a pump of soap from the empty plastic bottle at the sink. Water is a thin trickle from the faucet. I rinse my hands, then wipe them on my skirt.

He jerks his chin at the creaky steps I just came from. "Let's go."

A fresh surge of fear sends goose bumps scurrying across my skin, even the tiniest hairs at the back of my neck raising like antennae saluting danger.

I don't want to go back downstairs, to that dark hole of a closet, back to the other men. I don't want to feel the walls pressing in on me, to choke on the thick darkness that amplifies every fear living inside my mind.

But I have no weapon, not even a pair of shoes. I swallow my reservations and step out of the bathroom, moving slowly. All I have is my mind, my negotiating skills. I can do this.

"Please." I lower my voice to a whisper, cringing at the edge of desperation that clings to each syllable. "You don't have to do this. Let me go, now, and—"

"And what? You'll go back in time and convince your father not to play me against Cruz?" He gives a humorless laugh. "Cruz would kill me before I'd ever get a chance to testify against him."

"What if I could get you out of New York? Give you money to start over, somewhere else. Make a fresh start for yourself."

"There is no escape from Hugo Cruz."

"And you think Damon King is just going to let me go?"

He looks me up and down with a cold, appraising glance. "I think you're easily replaceable. Give it a couple of days and he'll forget all about you."

I want to argue, to protest.

But the truth is, I'm not entirely sure he's wrong. Without oxygen, the passion that raged between Damon and me will surely fade away. How long will it take before Damon decides I'm not worth the trouble?

Why shouldn't he give up on me, too?

chapter seven

Damon

"Did you get anything from that picture? Or the email?"

Computers pick up details the naked eye can't. Even though I hadn't noticed anything from my quick glance, I expected Finley would have some information by the time I got back to the office.

The swift shake of her head sends a crack through my chest. "Not yet."

"What about that damn dog walker? Or the dogs, the vans, the fucking trash on the street? Do we have anything to go on at all?"

"The second I do, I'll—"

The swell of my temper is a visceral thing, sending a hot and violent rage surging through my bloodstream like lava. "Fuck!" I slam my hand on the nearest flat surface. My palm makes a loud *thwack*, the reverberation shuddering through the bones of my arm. "There's gotta be something, damn it."

"We did learn something," she says. "We learned Cruz is contacting Lytton directly, without going through you."

My jaw is twitching from grinding my teeth. Finley is

right. I am the middle-man between Cruz and Granville, not Lytton. "If Lytton's trying to pull a fast one, let's get more eyes on the Manhattan DA's internal database."

I head for my office, my steps heavy with disappointment that Finley hasn't found something more concrete in my absence.

Using my servers, a fingerprint or photograph can be run through any database in the world. If Cruz's men are on an international or domestic watch list, we might get a hit in minutes.

I've assembled a brilliant, highly qualified team accustomed to working outside the box. Surely Aislinn should have been found by now.

It's already been hours.

From my own bank of computers, I check Finley's work. Every search function. Every set of parameters. Every source code, subnet address, and security network.

Sweat beads on my brow as I meticulously review every damn thing Finley has done to track down Aislinn.

"Find what you're looking for?"

I glance up to find her standing in my doorway, arms crossed as she leans against the wall, her face an impassive mask. "What do you think I'm looking for?"

"Proof that I'm not doing my job. Or that I'm stalling. Maybe even planting evidence to lead you in the wrong direction." She shrugs her shoulders. "Sabotage."

"Will I find it?"

"Have you?" she shoots back.

I push my chair back. "No."

It is the truth. Finley's work is above reproach.

"Did you really expect to find anything different?"

I don't answer. I am a desperate man, desperate for the truth. The truth is: hope outweighs expectation. I *wanted* to find errors in her work, whether intentional or not.

Because I need something to work with, something to fix. Something to do besides losing my goddamn mind.

Instead, I ask, "Are you doing everything you can to find her?"

Finley's eyes slide away from mine, but not in a deceptive way. It is because her expression softens. "Aislinn tried to get to know me. Not just as a way to work herself into your life or your business. I think she was genuinely interested in me, you know?"

I kick my legs out in front of my chair, crossing them at the ankles as I tip my head back and drag my palms over my face. A heavy sigh shudders from my lungs. "Yeah. I know."

Finley adds, "I'm ready to get to know her too. I want to. And not just because she's my sister."

"Half-sister," I correct, a teasing note just barely audible in a voice that is rough with worry.

"Whatever. I want her back, Damon. Same as you."

No one wants Aislinn back as badly as I do, but I'm not about to argue the point. It's a weight off my shoulders to know that Finley and I are driving for the same goal.

I stand up and walk toward her now, clapping a hand on her shoulder and giving a light squeeze. "I'm heading out, going to see what I can find out on the ground. You'll keep me updated."

My gut clenches when I get close enough to look into her eyes. They are identical to Aislinn's.

Identical, and yet entirely different.

Finley regards me with quiet, steady intelligence. Our relationship is based on history and mutual respect. She's been integral to the success of my business and to The Network. Our exchanges are cool and productive.

There are no sparks between Finley and me.

There never have been.

With Aislinn, we are our own fireworks show.

Everything between us is a clash, a blazing battle of wills and wants. Our energy and ideas. Our approach to work and life. Our passion for each other.

She drives me crazy with her questions and doubts and conflict.

And I fucking love the challenge.

Aislinn makes me feel alive in the most intense way.

The thought of never seeing her again, never fighting or kissing or laughing or fucking or—

No. I'm not going down that path.

I will get her back.

"Where are you going?"

The belly of the beast. "Uptown."

She blinks. "Los Muertos territory."

"While I'm gone, pull together a list of every art gallery and private collector Sebastián Cruz has ever done business with."

I've already dug into Cruz's personal financials. Everything appeared clean. But maybe I shouldn't be looking at them from his perspective. "Comb through their accounts. If they've ever received a single peso of Los Muertos cash, I want to know."

"Consider it done."

I stride past her and catch Burke's eye. "Ready to kick some Los Muertos ass?" I ask, cracking my knuckles.

His face splits into a wide grin. "Fuck, yeah."

"Let's roll."

Aislinn, I'm coming for you. The king will take back his queen. Check. Fucking. Mate.

chapter eight

Aislinn

It's been three days. The longest three days of my life.

No natural light penetrates the large closet, or maybe small storage room of this dark, dank basement, but I mark time by whether the food tossed my way is called lunch or dinner.

I did attempt a hunger strike, but by the second day, the dog walker, whose name I now know is Michael, said if I didn't eat something he would need to run errands for the rest of the day, leaving me alone with his three *compadres*.

I hated giving in.

Hated the sneer of satisfaction that made me feel as greasy as the fried dough of the foil-wrapped empanada Michael chucked my way.

I hated myself most of all. For still being here.

Michael took away my chair, so I've spent three days sitting on a crib-sized mattress, my back wedged into the corner, my knees tucked under my chin, my arms wrapped around my shins. I barely move. I barely breathe. I barely sleep.

I listen. Alert for any opportunity to escape.

So far, there hasn't been any.

But not a second has passed that I haven't been grateful to Damon for our last night together. For all our moments together, but particularly our last. Because that night is saving me now. The night I asked him to be my monster. *Prove to me that giving up control isn't the same as having it taken away.*

I have no control over anything right now, but when the darkness feels overwhelming, I close my eyes and remember the night it wasn't. I remember the intimacy of those hours. The feeling that Damon and I were the only two people in the universe.

And I pretend I'm still in his arms, safe inside our dark cocoon.

The darkness isn't quite as thick today. The door separating me from my captors is old and warped, difficult to close. Michael had been careless earlier when he brought me lunch.

A late lunch because my stomach was growling by the time he tossed me a greasy KFC bag. I'm nibbling on a drumstick when I hear footsteps on the stairs.

Footsteps that can't belong to one of my kidnappers, because all four of them are seated around the card table.

My heart leaps with joy, with relief.

The hell with all my ideas. Fairy tales are the bomb. Getting rescued by Damon King, my dark knight, my Prince Charming—what's wrong with that?

Nothing. Not a damn thing.

Excitement flares with each step. Michael and all his men, they are just walking corpses. Damon will crack their heads together. He'll split their throats. He'll snap their necks. I will stomp on their broken bodies. Spit in their bloody faces. We will walk out of here together.

I am certain those texts were just a misunderstanding.

Damon is not a hired assassin, taking orders from Chad and my father. I was angry because of what I read and he was angry because what I read was on his phone.

As Marisol used to tell me, "Two wrongs don't make a right."

Our two wrongs took us in the wrong direction, and I am eager to clear the air with Damon.

I still want to get away from New York. Away from my father and Chad. Away from Los Muertos. But I want to get back to Damon more.

I press my face against the narrow opening, my eyelashes brushing the edge of the door with each blink, impatiently waiting for my first glimpse of Damon in three days.

I can't wait to jump in Damon's arms and—

No. No, no, no.

The footsteps don't belong to Damon.

My heart sinks, dissolving at my feet as dread blows through me like an arctic wind. "Sebastián." I jerk back, whispering his name as a haze of tears clouds my vision. "No."

I haven't wanted to think he might be involved in this. The Sebastián Cruz I knew wasn't the son of a cartel kingpin. He was a nice kid. A childhood fling that went nowhere. A pleasant, but faded memory.

I force myself to look through the small opening again. Even in the dim light of the basement, the gold flecks inside Sebastián's pale green eyes shine brightly. He looks like he's made a wrong turn at the end of a runway, all immaculate clothes and perfect hair. The high sweep of his cheekbones leading to a strong chin, the perfect posture that conveys both arrogance and derision in equal measure. He pauses at the bottom step for a moment, inclining his head toward Michael and the other three men. "Where is she?"

Michael jerks his chin in my direction. "In there."

Sebastián sighs, whether in disappointment or anger, I can't tell. I hope it's the latter. I hope all of this has been a surprise to him and he's here to apologize and let me go.

"Stand at the top of the stairs, just in case she tries to run."

I gasp, feeling like I've been punched in the stomach. Sebastián may not have grabbed me off the street—but he is definitely one of my kidnappers.

The door opens and Sebastián peers inside, his face arranged into an artful mask of concern.

But a mask is all it is. If Sebastián were concerned for me, he would never have allowed this.

My fingers curl around the fried drumstick in my hands, tempted to chuck it at Sebastián and make a run for it. Except that there's nowhere to run. My would-be rapists are walking up the only set of stairs and have been tasked—by Sebastián—with blocking my exit.

But there's no running away from the betrayal that wraps around my lungs, constricting them. The chicken leg drops to the ground from my numb fingers. "What have you done?"

He looks around, disappointment pulling at his brow as he takes in our surroundings. "You won't have to stay here much longer, Aislinn. Just until King is convinced that I'm not—"

"Sebastián!" I interrupt, shouting his name this time. "What the hell is going on?"

He gestures toward the card table and folding chairs.

I don't want to sit. I want to march right up the stairs and out the door to ... wherever we are.

But I squash the instinct and sit down, flicking a tongue over my dry lips and pasting the interested yet aloof expression I use when meeting with new clients on my face. An expression that says: *nothing you can possibly say will shock me, so tell me everything.*

Sebastián lifts his eyes to mine. "Do you remember what I said to you when we were paired up in Biology—the day we had to dissect a frog?"

I blink away my surprise, although the twang of impatience is harder to hide. "I'm not exactly in the mood to reminisce about high school."

"Humor me."

I remember. Of course, I remember. "You said I have nice hands, I should keep them clean."

He nods. "I thought I could keep my hands clean too. But when you're born into Los Muertos, it's next to impossible. There's a chance though. A chance for both of us."

For a moment neither of us says anything, but then I lift my arms, gesturing at the basement I've been stuck in for three days. "That's it—you expect me to buy that cryptic explanation? Are you kidding me, Seb?"

He shakes his head firmly. "I wish I was."

"I call bullshit." Tears sting my eyes. "Let me go, Seb. Let's walk upstairs together. Let's get out of here."

Through the wet haze clouding my vision, I see Sebastián frown. "I can't. Not yet."

"Why not?" I plead.

"Because this time, I need your help. And believe it or not, you're safer here."

The stress and anxiety that have battered me like twin tides finally crest over my head. "Safer? How? I was taken off the street, drugged, shoved in a van, and threatened. I've been kept against my will for three days with four men who have made it all too clear what they would rather be doing with me."

Sebastián's lips flatten, his stare turning fierce. "If they touch you, I will kill them."

"Just get me out of here."

"Soon, I promise."

He stands up to go and I grab for his hand, hysteria bubbling up inside my chest. "If you can't take me with you, then stay. Don't leave me here." I don't trust the men who have been assigned to watch me, and at least with Sebastián, I feel like I have a chance at convincing him to let me go.

"I will come back. And I'll explain everything."

"When?"

"Tonight. I'll come back tonight, after dark."

"At least … At least tell me where I am. Mexico? Or maybe somewhere in the mountains?" In all likelihood, my location doesn't matter. But the not knowing is driving me crazy.

Sebastián looks puzzled by the options I've thrown out. "Neither. You're still in New York."

"New York? But, I don't hear any traffic. Not a single siren." I thought I heard the laugh of a child earlier, on my last trip to the bathroom. But Michael had hustled me back downstairs so quickly I couldn't be sure.

"This is a chapel built on the grounds of The Cloisters. It was originally intended as an exhibit, but it became something of a storage shed before it was ever opened to the public."

"The Cloisters? You mean, the museum in the Bronx?"

He nods once and gets to his feet, pressing a kiss to my cheek as he straightens. "But I have to go. We close in an hour and I need to lock up my office. I'll come back later."

I force myself not to pull away, or rub away the echo of his touch. "You'll return tonight." It's not a question.

"In a few hours, I promise. I'll explain more then."

That's two promises in the span of as many minutes.

I wish I believed either of them.

chapter nine

Damon

I've hit a dead end.

It's been three days.

Days.

I have tracked down every lead, followed every trail, questioned every source.

My knuckles are bruised and bloody from men who have lied to me, or stupidly refused to answer my questions the first time they were asked. My emotions are running too hot, and they are too close to the surface.

Every sentence sounds like a lie, every conversation like an elaborate deception.

Whether I am being stonewalled or deceived or there is truly no information to be gained—I can't tell anymore.

But I haven't relied solely on human sources.

I've combed through the dark net with meticulous care. I've tracked money, chased chatter, stalked like a hunter. I'm not hampered by privacy laws or insufficient budgets.

My eyeballs ache from lack of sleep and overexposure to the harsh light of computer screens.

And yet, I still haven't found Aislinn.

There have been hits from facial recognition and criminal databases. Hours spent on electronic surveillance and chasing down family members and known associates.

So far, they've all been false leads.

I am no closer to finding Aislinn than I was when Finley walked into my bathroom.

At the sound of a sharp rap on my open door, I look up to find Burke's wide shoulders and unsmiling face filling the opening. I'm in my office, the shirt I wear stained with the blood of yet another Los Muertos soldier. "Is it done?"

Burke gives a curt nod. "Yes. Surveillance equipment was successfully installed in Sebastián Cruz's apartment an hour ago. No red flags yet."

I can't shake the sense that Sebastián Cruz is involved, despite the lack of any evidence.

Hacking has its limitations. I've had a team on Cruz since he showed up at the award dinner honoring James Granville, and I've gotten as far as I can with his online presence. There's been no suspicious activity on his phone or computers, but I need more eyes.

Is he using burners? Meeting with people posing as staff or delivering food?

To get access to Cruz's apartment, I've disabled some internal systems in his high tech building. Maintenance calls were rerouted and, conveniently, I sent in my own people to act as technicians and repair the problem. "What about activity outside of his apartment? Has he gone anywhere else we should check out?"

"Not really. I thought we were onto something when he headed to the Bronx this afternoon, but turns out, he was only going to that museum up there."

"The Cloisters?"

Burke nods.

A branch of the Metropolitan Museum of Art, The Cloisters was designed to resemble a medieval European monastery and display art from that time period. While The Met is located on the Upper East Side, The Cloisters is more of a buck-toothed, brace-faced stepchild relegated to the Bronx, a borough most Manhattanites will never set foot in.

Sebastián Cruz curates the museum's collection of illuminated manuscripts.

I've already posed as a potential collector at every gallery Cruz has worked with in the past six months.

Running my hands through my hair, I groan. "You think there's a chance in hell he's in the dark on this?"

Burke lifts a shoulder. "His art world circles are about as far from Los Muertos territory as you can get."

"Except that The Cloisters are in the Bronx. That *is* Los Muertos territory." I haul myself to my feet. "Come on. Let's go to check out some medieval art."

If Sebastián Cruz is behind Aislinn's abduction, not even a forged iron breastplate will prevent me from ripping his heart from his chest.

"You sure about this?"

I glance at Burke as I push a couple of bills across the ticket desk. We are in the main hall of The Cloisters. Stone walls rise up around us, half a dozen tall archways leading to various wings and exhibitions. A grandmotherly looking woman exchanges my cash for two folded museum guides. "Don't miss the Unicorn Tapestries. They are glorious."

There is no fee for New York residents, but I'm not about

to whip out identification. I don't care about the money, and Burke and I already stand out from this crowd of mostly college-age art freaks and stroller-pushing families. There's no reason to leave our names too.

"Wouldn't miss them," I lie, handing Burke one of the brochures and managing an appreciative smile.

I'm not here to sightsee. The priceless series of tapestries depicting a group of hunters pursuing a unicorn is of no interest to me.

I'm too preoccupied hunting my own unicorn. Aislinn Granville.

Sidestepping a toddler with a runny nose and a leaking sippy cup, I grumble, "Illuminated manuscripts are downstairs. Let's go."

We break left and wander through several rooms marked by dreary art and brightly stained glass windows. A staircase leads to the ground floor and we follow signs to the Treasury Room. Technically, it is two rooms. The larger one displays carvings and jewelry while the smaller, rectangular space holds the manuscripts.

Although I have researched Cruz's area of expertise, this is my first time seeing a manuscript in person. Some cases display entire books while others only hold brittle, yellowing pieces of paper covered in faded script and odd drawings.

Burke and I make our way through the room, silently peering into each case and reading every exhibit label. I'm trying to soak up some grain of knowledge that will get me into Cruz's head. When we finally get to the last one, Burke grunts and looks up at me. "I wasn't sure before, but I am now. He's gotta be involved."

"And which manuscript told you that?"

"All of them. Boss, if these old books are the only thing in his life, he'd be dead of boredom already."

I don't disagree with him. "I need air."

We walk through the actual cloisters, which are really just courtyards, and then the outdoor gardens. The grounds are thrown into shadow from the descending sun, the Hudson River a silver-gray smudge separating land from sky.

I turn in a slow circle, looking for … I don't know what.

"Let's head back inside, hunt down Cruz." He has to have an office somewhere.

Burke grunts. "Don't think we need to do that." At my frown, he jerks his chin toward the river.

Walking through the manicured gardens is Sebastián Cruz himself. Our eyes meet when we're still thirty feet from each other, but even at a distance, I don't miss the quick flash of discomfort he covers with a stilted prep school smirk. "Injecting some culture into your life, King?"

I don't bother with pleasantries. "Where is she?"

"If you're looking for the Mona Lisa, I'm afraid you've come to the wrong—"

I step in close to him, toe to toe. "In case you haven't noticed, Los Muertos soldiers are disappearing lately. I wasn't planning on killing the prince, but I'm losing my patience. Where. The Fuck. Is Aislinn?"

Sebastián doesn't blink. "You just don't get it. The best thing you can do for her is to stop looking. Granville's daughter will never be yours."

Because you don't deserve her.

That last bit is unspoken, but it blares inside my ears as if Sebastián were using a megaphone.

"You're a fucking dead man, Cruz." I am going to strangle the life out of him with my bare hands. It is only the chatter of children around us that prevents me from doing just that.

"We both are." He arches a brow at me. "But I'm quite certain you'll already be waiting for me when I arrive in Hell."

With a parting nod at Burke, he strolls off and only a steadying hand on my forearm prevents me from chasing him down. "That fuck knows where she is." I'm certain of it.

"I agree."

I spin back around, scanning the direction Cruz came from. Finally, something catches my attention. "Do you see that?"

Burke follows the trajectory of my pointed finger. At the edge of the gardens, leading into the larger Fort Tryon Park, a cropping of trees seems to be shielding another building. "The cottage?"

I shake my head. Fort Tryon cottage was built as a gatehouse for the former owners of the property. Now it is used by the New York City Parks Department. "No. The cottage is farther north."

Veering off the manicured path, we walk toward the copse of trees. "Looks like a church."

A decrepit, abandoned church—or chapel, given its small dimensions. I pull out my guidebook. "This isn't on the map."

Burke rattles the doorknob. "Locked. Should I pick it?"

I turn around. There are still people exploring the grounds less than a hundred yards away. "Let's try to see inside first."

Burke and I split off in opposite directions, peering through the windows. The place is a fucking mess. It looks like a storage unit for the kind of art displayed in The Cloisters. Art that has been irreparably broken.

There's no sign of Aislinn or Los Muertos soldiers.

We meet back up by the front doors. "What do you think? Should we bother looking inside?"

I exhale a frustrated breath, looking from Burke up to the hulking Cloisters that rise from the craggy landscape like a medieval fortress. I can practically feel Cruz's eyes on me.

I look at the door again, at the heavy handle that's not nearly as dirty as the windows. Someone has been here recently—although probably just to dump off a broken statue. Still, it is worth a shot.

"Yeah. Let's do it." I reach in my pocket for the small set of tools I always carry with me.

"… This looks like a perfect spot, doesn't it? Sit down, and I'll tell you a story about a wicked king, a beautiful princess, and the prince who battled a beast to win her love."

Burke stiffens and I spin around. Beneath the shade of a nearby tree, a dozen kids plop down on the grass, arranging themselves in a semi-circle around a woman holding a picture book. Several sets of parents accompany them. No trees shield us from this angle. If I break in now, we'll have an audience.

"Fuck," I mutter, shoving my kit back in my pocket just as the woman holding the book lifts her hand in an enthusiastic wave. "Let's come back later, after dark."

chapter ten

Aislinn

It's been hours and Seb still hasn't returned.

Disappointment is a vice around my ribs, so tight I can hear them cracking from strain. Each breath is a struggle. Each sigh is a sound of defeat.

I should be used to disappointment by now. Accustomed to the ache of broken promises.

But I am not.

Tonight, I'm handed a milkshake with my dinner. It is a poor consolation prize for freedom, but I suck it down greedily, long angry pulls from the straw. I am going stir crazy here, with nothing to occupy me. I've already read the paper Michael tossed at me earlier. Cover to cover. Not even the advertisements and classified ads have gone unexamined as I crouched by the thin strip of light coming through the swollen door.

Maybe especially the classified ads. I hadn't realized that, in this age of Craig's List and Facebook tag sale groups, they still exist at all. I've taken some small measure of comfort in reading about the lakefront cabin in Maine, offering fishing and boating and summer camp options for the busy Manhattan family to escape to on weekends or for the entire summer, and a free weekly knitting class at a Williamsburg yarn store.

Maybe I'll live long enough to knit by a lake.

The straw gives a final gurgle and I drop the empty cup, lifting my hands to my temples with a groan. *Ugh. Brain freeze.*

Except ... it isn't.

My arms barely make it to my shoulders before falling limply to my lap. Michael, who yanks open the door when he hears the cup drop, catches me as I list to the side, nearly toppling off my chair.

I open my mouth to protest, but my tongue won't cooperate. Even my eyelids are too heavy to hold a glare. They slam shut just as I hear one of the other men chortle, "Let's fuck her now. No one will know, not even her."

I never should have drunk that damn milkshake.

chapter eleven

Damon

I've been sitting in Granville's home office for nearly two hours when he finally comes through the door. Impatience thrums just beneath my skin; I am anxious to return to The Cloisters with Burke and break into the dilapidated chapel. I don't expect to find much, but it's a lead worth exploring.

Even so, I wait until he pours himself a Scotch, downs half of it and then tops up his glass again.

And then I pull the chain of his desk lamp, revealing my presence.

Granville jumps, spilling liquor all over his suit. "Goddamn it, King," he howls, setting down his glass and swatting at his chest. "What are you doing here?"

"We had a deal. I clean up your mess and take care of your daughter while I do it."

"Yeah? Well, apparently, she's someone else's problem now. You should be grateful. I know I am."

"Grateful?"

He glares at me and returns to the bar, pouring himself a fresh drink. "Yes, grateful. Like me, you have more important things to worry about."

There is nothing more important to me than Aislinn. "What would those be?" I prod, getting the same ominous vibe from Granville as I did from Lytton just a few days ago.

He takes a sip of his drink and ignores the question. "All this interest in my bastard daughter." He grunts. "Who knew?"

I bite down on my urge to throttle him. "What kind of interest?"

He finishes his scotch, swaying a bit on his feet as he grabs the bottle by the neck and sets it on his desk. Dropping into the chair opposite me, the one normally reserved for visitors but is the only option currently available, he refills his glass again. It is obvious that these aren't his first drinks of the night.

I don't mind. Liquor loosens the tongue.

I lean back in his chair and cross my feet on a corner of his desk. "What kind of interest, Granville?" I repeat.

"Nothing you would know anything about."

"Try me."

"Fine." He belches then pats his chest. "Wedding bells, if you must know. I had my heart set on Chad, though. That boy is going to make a fine politician. Looks like a Kennedy, and Aislinn would make a great Jackie. Their wedding would have been the perfect kick-off to my campaign, the start of a new political legacy."

My blood heats at the thought of Aislinn and Chad together, but I manage to keep my temper in check. "And now that's not happening?"

"Doesn't look that way anymore. Hugo Cruz has made me an offer." He swills the amber liquid in his glass, a giddy laugh leaking from his lips. "An offer I can't refuse."

chapter twelve

Aislinn

When I wake up, I'm not lying on a thin, lumpy cot that smells of mildew and urine, with only my elbow to cushion my head. The blanket wrapped tightly around my shoulders isn't threadbare and damp, completely ineffectual against the wet, drafty basement.

Instead, my head is nestled into a fluffy pillow, the mattress beneath me a luxurious cloud. I am cocooned within a thick duvet that smells of talc and lavender.

I sigh happily, warm and cozy, snuggling deeper as I push aside my strange dreams. Sebastián and Michael. Syringes and milkshakes. Dogs, duct tape, damp basements, dirty bathrooms.

All of it was just a dream. An awful, unrelenting nightmare.

"Thank God," I mutter groggily.

"You're awake."

My eyelids fly open, my hands fisting the covers against my neck.

That voice didn't come from my unconscious. And I am

not in a basement … but I am not in Damon's bedroom, either.

With my heart in my throat, I turn my head to find Sebastián perched on the end of the bed, staring at me with an air of impatience.

Reality slams into me like thunder. My location may have changed, but my nightmare was real. Is real.

Because I am still living it.

I run my tongue over dry lips, fighting the pang of nausea that twists my stomach. There is so much I want to say, and an anguished scream is gathering strength at the back of my throat, fighting for release.

My brain is on fire, a quiet fury simultaneously thickening and heating the blood inside my veins so that it oozes at a sluggish pace beneath my skin. After a long moment, all I say is, "You never came."

"Plans changed." Sebastián is unrepentant, maddeningly so. "It made more sense to bring you here."

My eyes bounce around the unfamiliar room. Gold-framed art adorns yellow walls, thick crown molding emphasizes the high ceilings, ornate window treatments cling to mullioned windows. The decor is elegant and formal, like a bed-and-breakfast at a historic country manor. "Where is *here?*"

"This is the country home of a client of mine. I curated his collection last year and I still swing by occasionally. He's out of town right now." Sebastián lifts a hand and lightly sets it down on my duvet-covered hip. "After I left you yesterday," he pauses for a moment, "I decided that your accommodations, while convenient, were unsuitable. This is a much better place for us to talk. Reconnect."

Reconnect? What I want is a phone, or access to the Internet. Car keys. An unlocked door.

Freedom.

"Are we still in the city?"

He shakes his head. "No, but not far. Westchester County."

A cage is still a cage. "Why, Sebastián? You still haven't explained anything."

His expression tightens. "Take a shower and come downstairs. I know how to make a decent omelet and then we'll go for a walk. We have a lot to discuss."

The thought of a shower is enough to make the barrage of questions retreat behind my teeth.

I am filthy.

But I don't immediately race to the bathroom. After Sebastián closes the door behind him, I jump out of bed to stare out the windows.

This isn't just a house. It's an estate. One with acres and acres of land.

Both windows are locked, the thin white wire snaking around the frame evidence of an alarm. Whether it would alert the police or Hugo Cruz, I don't know. Either way, there's no balcony, just a long drop down. Breaking my legs would seriously hamper any chance of escape.

I'm not even sure escape is a possibility. I don't see a single neighbor. No road to run toward.

I open each drawer of the heavy bombe chests that bracket the bed. Empty. Same for the enormous dresser on the opposite wall.

I have better luck in the bathroom.

A small manicure set that includes a pair of cuticle scissors.

I set it on the ledge of the shower and start the water, waiting until it runs hot to take off my clothes.

It's then that I recall what one of the men said, just before I passed out. *Let's fuck her now. No one will know, not even her.*

Fighting back a wave of panic, I examine my naked body

in the mirror of the bathroom. My skin is peppered with bruises in varying shades of blue and green and yellow. But they are all in places where I recall being hurt. There are no fingerprints on my breasts or thighs, no chafing or soreness anywhere there shouldn't be.

Apparently raping an unconscious woman isn't enough of a lure to risk defying Michael. Or inviting the wrath of Hugo Cruz.

Exhaling a relieved breath, I step beneath the single showerhead and tip my head back. Water cascades down my hair and over my shoulders, taking with it a stream of fresh tears. They fall unchecked down my face, mixing with the spray sliding down my body, flowing into the drain.

Relief. Fear. Anger. Desperation. Regret. Longing. Frustration.

So many emotions. So many tears.

I am grateful for the certainty that the last man inside my body was Damon. But knowing how little control I have over that fact … is sickening.

Damon King—where are you? Are you looking for me?

Have you given up on me?

I press my palms against the shower wall, leaning my forehead against the tile as I suck in deep breaths of humid mist. It is tempting to slide down the wall, to stay within the warm enclosure until the water runs cold.

But then what?

How am I going to get out of here?

I turn off the water with shaking hands and dry my body with a thick white bath sheet before using it as a turban for my hair and slipping into a plush bathrobe hanging from a hook on the back of the bathroom door. I brush my teeth, staring at my reflection in the foggy mirror.

You can do this, Aislinn. You can convince Sebastián to let you go. And if you can't, you'll figure out how to get the hell out of here. Just

... don't give up. Don't ever give up.

It might not be the most inspired pep talk, but it will have to do.

I can't bear to put on the dirty outfit I've been wearing for days, and there are no other alternatives. With a shrug, I put the scissors into one of the deep pockets and fill up the sink with warm, sudsy water. The bloodstains have long since set. They don't come out of my ivory silk blouse, and there is nothing to be done about the tears to the fabric. Even so, I squeeze out the excess water and hang them to dry over the shower door.

My bare feet make no sound as I step into the hall and make my way down the wide, curving staircase and across the marble foyer. I want to run right out the front door, but a quick glance shows one of Cruz's men standing guard. His sinister smile and the bulge of his gun are strong deterrents.

Following the scent of eggs and coffee, I walk through an archway, down another hall, and into an enormous kitchen. I round the corner just as Sebastián is setting two full plates onto an ornately carved walnut table.

He pulls out a chair and I sit down, the bay window overlooking an immaculately kept lawn and gardens.

I could be a guest he's invited for the weekend. Old friends catching up over brunch.

But I'm not. The awkwardness of this situation is inescapable, and yet neither of us comments on it.

My nerves are drawn piano wire tight as I spread a napkin on my lap and pick up my fork. "You know, if you wanted to keep in touch, you could have just slid into my DMs." My voice is several octaves higher than normal, belying my attempt to keep things casual.

Even though this is Seb ... I'm still on shaky ground.

He forks a bite of eggs into his mouth, an unrepentant grin curving his lips. "Unfortunately, some things are out of my control."

I take a few bites myself, trying to figure out the best way to approach this conversation. "Can we start at the beginning—how did we get here, Seb? Beyond your father, what is your connection to Los Muertos?"

His rough chuckle is more pained than amused. *"Beyond my father?* Come on now, Aislinn. Can you separate your involvement in New York politics from James Granville?"

"I don't work for my father anymore. I quit."

At that, Seb tilts his head back and laughs. It is a deep, velvety sound, as rich as the coffee in my mug. "That's not exactly an option in my world. If you are born Los Muertos, you will die Los Muertos."

I wince at the finality of his words, the bitterness of his tone. But it doesn't lessen my rancor. "I have no affiliation with the cartel, or your family, and yet you left me with men who wouldn't have blinked at killing me—after they raped me, of course."

A muscle in his jaw tics. "They would have paid for it with their lives."

"So? Their death wouldn't erase their actions."

"Did they … do anything to you?"

"No," I shoot back. "But that's not the point."

"I think you're missing the point."

"Really?" I cross my arms. "Because from where I'm sitting, it looks like you're treating me with complete disregard, yet you expect my complete subservience. And, let me assure you, that particular mannerism is not one I'm familiar with."

He drops his fork with a clatter. "We've gotten off on the wrong foot. And I'm sorry for that, truly. Let's go back to the beginning, like you suggested. I believe you will understand my actions, even if you don't agree with them."

I could dig in my heels and argue until I'm blue in the

face, but that won't get me anywhere. Most importantly, it won't get me out of *here*. So I take a breath and compose my features into an aloof mask. "Back to the beginning it is. What brought you to New York all those years ago?"

"I'm a second son. I was brought here to be out of the line of fire, in case anything happened to my older brother. But over the years, New York has become a critical part of our business. Almost thirty percent of revenue. The distribution hub for our East Coast operations."

I am taken aback by his blasé attitude. Sebastián could be talking about coffee or oil or pencils. But he's not. His business is drugs and guns and who knows what else. Well, I'm sure *he* knows.

I don't want to know.

I push my plate away as the implications of his explanation spoil my breakfast. "What about your art appraisal work?"

"It's a legitimate interest of mine. And there was a time when I believed …" Sebastián pauses, clearing his throat. "It doesn't matter what I believed. Unfortunately, my work with illuminated manuscripts is now just a great cover."

A great cover. "The Seb I knew wouldn't have become a glorified drug dealer."

The look he gives me is old and weary. Disillusioned. "No. The Seb you knew—"

He stops abruptly, pushing his chair back. It squeals on the parquet floor. "How about that walk?"

I look down at my bare feet. "I don't have shoes."

With a wry grin, Seb toes off his own and extends his hand. "Come on, a little grass under our feet is just what we need."

chapter thirteen

Aislinn

$\mathcal{S}$ebastián and I walk across the stone patio and onto the lawn. The morning is cool and crisp, the grass wet with dew and springy beneath the arches of my feet. And after four days trapped in a damp basement, the fresh air is heavenly.

But it still doesn't change the fact that I'm being kept here. A fancy fortress, but still a prison. My body hums with anger.

Noticing the pensive expression on Sebastián's face, I ask, "Are we talking out here because you think we're being listened to inside the house?"

If he's surprised by my question, he doesn't show it. "I'm not sure, but it's a good guess."

I drag my feet through the grass, feeling the tickle of the blades between my toes. "What were you going to say in there?"

He sighs, running long fingers through his hair. "The kid you knew didn't realize that his last name was a curse. He thought he was free, that his future was his own."

My heart is not nearly as hardened as I want it to be. The

seditious organ aches at the sadness in his voice, the resignation etched into his face, the grimace twisting his lips. An ache only compounded by Sebastián's next statement.

"I was a fool."

I take his hand in mine. "You are not your father, Seb. You don't have to be a part of his business, you can walk away. If you want to."

He doesn't answer. We continue walking, hand in hand. Ten years ago, I would have been absolutely giddy.

But there is nothing sexual about our contact this morning. And despite the fresh air, I'm choking on the thick tension between us.

"Back in high school, when we started hanging out, my father found out who you were." He stops. "*Del tal palo, tal astilla.* Like father like—"

"—like son," I finish hesitantly, not knowing where he's going with this.

Dropping my hand, he squints up at the sky and rubs the back of his neck. "My father married a politician's daughter. That's how Los Muertos became the most powerful cartel in Mexico."

My stomach churns, making me regret even those few bites of breakfast. "What does that have to do with me?"

Sebastián returns his gaze to mine. "The way I see it— we're both imprisoned. By our fathers, by this city, by our last names."

The truth chafes at me. In New York, I will always be known as James Granville's daughter. "Go on."

"This kidnapping plot—you're not being used as leverage, like you thought." There is an almost manic pattern to his speech, a desperation in the blaze burning inside his eyes. "My father wants to use his money and muscle to make your father the most powerful man in New York, and eventually, the country."

I narrow my eyes. "In exchange for what?"

"His private support and public ignorance of Los Muertos operations."

"From what I've learned, it sounds like a deal my father would jump at."

"Which is why my father wants a guarantee. If there was a connection between our families, if we are actually family, my father would be more confident of the long-term prospects."

"Family ..." The implications of Sebastián's explanation sinks into my brain. "As in marriage? Between us?"

"Exactly."

"Your father had me kidnapped off the street, drugged, bound, threatened by four of his thugs, locked inside a church basement for four days—and now he expects me to become his daughter-in-law?" Hysterical laughter bubbles up in my throat as the absurd reality of my situation finally hits home.

"I know it sounds crazy. But there's a way out if we team up together."

"No." I poke my finger into his chest for emphasis. I am so tired of being used by men. Expected to advance their interests without any thought of my own. "*You* understand— I'm not getting married to appease your father or mine. I am not some Barbie doll bride to be paired off with a convenient Ken doll."

Whirling around, I stomp away from Sebastián and his outrageous proposition.

Marriage.

No way.

Not long ago, I considered marrying Chad for similar reasons.

But they were *my* reasons.

Our relationship was convenient and comfortable.

Mutually beneficial.

Dating in Manhattan is like running a gauntlet of egotistical bankers, alcoholic lawyers, aspiring artists, and tourists just looking for a story to take home. A gauntlet I happily avoided, because I had Chad.

But then Damon King showed up and upended my world. He taught me all about passion. How it whispered through my veins in the most delicious way, setting my skin on fire. The explosive power of an orgasm that couldn't be replicated by a battery-operated toy.

Not that King is marriage material. Or that the spark between us could last a lifetime.

But if I've learned anything from him, it is not to sell myself short by settling for convenience.

Especially someone else's convenience.

Before I can get far, Sebastián grabs my wrist and pulls me back. "What if a simple *I do* means we can live our lives as we see fit? I don't want to be involved in Los Muertos any more than you want to work for your father. We can leave here, travel the world. Live *our* lives, not *theirs*."

Sebastián's reasoning is eerily similar to my thoughts as I walked away from Damon three—no, four days ago. All I wanted was to get away from New York and leave everything and everyone behind.

Sure, I would miss my mother. And I would miss Marisol. But the rest of it ... the expectations and obligations and threats.

Nope.

I don't want to acknowledge the truth in Seb's theory. But I can't deny it.

"So," I question him, "love has no place in your marriage, then?"

Sebastián scoffs. "Love? Come on, Aislinn. What you and I have is better. We understand each other." His face softens and he sweeps a knuckle beneath my chin. "I think it's best if we keep emotion out of this. Establish a business arrangement."

I hesitate. Sebastián's proposal makes sense. He's offering me exactly what I thought I wanted. What I'd been perfectly willing to settle for. Before.

It's no longer enough. Not anymore.

I need passion. Intensity.

Love.

"No. Tell your father to leave me alone. I want nothing to do with his plans for world domination. And I won't be dominated, either."

I'm halfway back to the house when Sebastián calls my name. "I heard about the bruises on your wrists and ankles. Sounds to me like domination is exactly what you're into."

I spin and walk through the grass until our bare feet are just inches apart. "We haven't seen or spoken to each other in ten years. Don't presume to know anything about me."

"I stayed away from you for your own good, Aislinn." Sadness pulls at the corners of his lips. "But it was too late, the damage was done. My father has been planning this for years. It is our fate."

chapter fourteen

Aislinn

I stomp away from Sebastián. There's too much anger and frustration rattling around inside my chest to bear the thought of going back inside. Willingly returning to my cage.

Instead, I edge around the house, getting my first view of the front. Like the back, an endless expanse of grass stretches as far as the eye can see, but here it is split by a long driveway that leads to an oval courtyard. It's been filled in with tiny white stones that sparkle beneath the sunshine like an iridescent pond. After a few steps, the rough edges scratch the smooth soles of my feet as if I'm walking on crushed glass.

"Stupid stones," I mutter, hopping back onto the luxurious lawn. I circle the house several times, crossing the front yard by walking across the narrow Belgian block bricks. There is a wide flagstone path I could use, but I don't. Instead, I concentrate on my balance, on putting one foot in front of the other, without falling, without so much as a wobble. It's an oddly soothing exercise.

I don't see Michael, but I do catch sight of Carlos's men

as I roam around the grounds. They don't say anything to me, but from the way their sunglass-covered eyes track my steps, I'm sure that if I took off running, I would be tackled to the ground in minutes.

The illusion of freedom is just as abrasive as the obvious absence of it. At least in the basement, I knew I was being held captive. Here, I can run and jump and scream—but I cannot escape.

Sebastián is watching me, too. I saw him from the corner of my eye, looking down at me through a window at the back of the house.

His forehead rests against the glass pane, his hooded eyes and pensive scowl giving the impression that he feels just as trapped as I do.

The sun is almost directly overhead, and I am warm in the heavy robe as I meet his eyes. I am about to jog up the back stairs when Sebastián comes down. "What's your end game here?" I ask. "I haven't seen you since the day we graduated and now you expect me to believe you're on my side."

"I am on your side."

"Prove it. Let me go."

He shakes his head slowly. "Don't you see—if I let you go, you're just returning to captivity. But together, we can be free. I'm offering you a new life, Aislinn. You can make your own rules. Do what you want, when you want."

"That doesn't sound like a marriage."

"Sure, it does. In name only."

I tell myself not to be offended that Sebastián barely hints at commitment to any degree and to consider his offer with an open mind. What is tying me to New York? My mother probably won't realize I'm gone. And my father definitely won't care.

A new life. Somewhere, anywhere.

It is tempting.

And I am tempted.

For a moment. A very long moment.

What would it be like to start over? To not be known as *Aislinn Granville, James Granville's daughter.* I could go back to school, study …

My mind draws a blank. Given the choice to do anything, I don't know where to start.

Think, Aislinn. What would make me wake up with a smile on my face?

Damon.

The answer is immediate. And so painful a hand flies up to my mouth to stifle a cry.

The last time I smiled was the last morning I woke up in Damon's bed.

It's been days. Is he still looking for me? Does he miss me?

Before I saw Chad's texts, I'd been happy. More than just happy. I'd been content.

I had rolled over and pressed my face into his pillow. Breathing in the scent of whiskey and wood and pure, ambrosial masculinity. *Eau de Damon.*

If I take Sebastián up on his offer, if I leave, I will never wake up in Damon's bed again. I will never kiss him again or smell him again or be bent over a table by him again. There will be no more battle of wills or verbal sparring.

Do I want a life without my dark king?

No. Hell, no.

With a jolt, I realize that I do have something keeping me here, something to stay and fight for. Someone.

Damon King.

My devil. My monster. Mine.

"I'm sorry that I can't be the one to help you escape from your cage, Sebastián. I am. No matter where I go—I'll wish I was with Damon."

"He is not as powerful as he thinks he is. In fact, King's about to be dethroned." He chuckles. "I almost felt sorry for the poor bastard when I ran into him yesterday."

I gasp. "Yesterday? You saw Damon yesterday?"

He frowns, a vein pulsing at the edge of his temple. "I wouldn't read too much into it, Aislinn. He can't offer you what I'm offering—freedom."

"I don't care," I screech, finally losing my temper. "Where? What did he say?"

"He came to see me, at The Cloisters."

Hope strengthens the tattered remnants of my composure as understanding finally dawns. "And that's why you moved me."

A reluctant "Yes" makes it through Sebastián's pursed lips. "But, Aislinn, use your head. King can't win against Los Muertos."

I don't care about some battle with a drug lord. I'm preoccupied by the proof that Damon hasn't forgotten about me. He's still looking for me. The flame of passion that ignited between us hasn't burned out.

I can't give up on King. I won't.

A decision that has come solely from my heart.

An organ that shudders inside my chest when Sebastián adds, "Whether you go back to him or not, Damon King's days are numbered."

I choke on a breath. "What?"

"King has built his empire on cryptocurrency mining. Controlling crime is just a side hustle for him. And because he's one of the richest men in the world, in completely untraceable currency, he has almost limitless influence and power. But my father has finally infiltrated his organization. Once he gets access to his accounts, King is as good as dead."

"He's … *what?*"

Sebastián's gaze turns suspicious. "I shouldn't have told you."

"But you did." My voice is a hushed whisper as I stare at him, trying to convince myself that his defiant, almost prideful expression doesn't mean what I know it does.

Damon has a mole.

My knees feel like they're about to buckle. I need to get back to him. Immediately.

I spin away from Sebastián, chewing on an already ragged cuticle and trying to figure out what I can say to make that happen. "If I agree to your terms, what then? We can leave?"

"Then we get married."

"Today, in front of the goons your father hired?" I will agree to anything if it means returning to Damon. I have to warn him. Save him.

"No, of course not." He reaches his hand out for mine. "It will be the kind of wedding you deserve. We'll invite everyone who's anyone. How about the Plaza, or the St. Regis?"

That kind of wedding will take months of planning.

Hope flutters on tentative wings. "Fine," I say quickly. "Tell your father I agree and let's get out of here. Or just give me a phone. I can start calling around, interviewing wedding planners." *Give me a phone so I can call Damon.*

Sebastián chuckles. "I sent Michael and one of the men into town to pick up some supplies and clothes for you. When they return, I'll have them get a message to my father and start coordinating our return to New York."

"Why can't we just leave now?"

"Because this is my cage too. I can't bring you back to New York unless my father approves it. And because of King's stranglehold on our communications, we can't just pick up the phone and call him. It's going to take time."

Time Damon may not have. I stumble to the nearest chair

and fall into it, taking deep breaths until I can look up at Sebastián again. "How long will it take?"

He shrugs. "A few days."

"What about your client? Won't he come back soon?"

"Not for weeks yet. And his caretaker has been persuaded to take an extended vacation."

Sharp little daggers of anxiety attack my lungs with each indrawn breath. I struggle to my feet, hauling myself up the stairs with the help of the banister. It's not until I reach the second-floor landing that I decide to explore the house while I have a chance.

I walk past the door of the bedroom I woke up in and keep going. I have to find a way out of here.

I race from bedroom to bedroom—looking for a phone or a way to escape without breaking my neck. I find a phone … but there is no dial tone.

Disappointment crashes into me like thunder, but I push through it. Emotions are a luxury I can't afford right now.

I hit pay dirt on the third bedroom. A balcony!

With my heart in my throat, I pull at the handle.

It's not locked.

I hesitate for just a second, expecting an alarm to blare, or one of Cruz's men to appear. But neither of those things happens.

I slip outside quietly, tightening the belt of my robe and peering over the edge. I am directly above the stone patio. Too high to jump, even if I dangle from the railing.

But just to the right is a pediment that extends over a window. It's several feet lower than the balcony.

My pulse is roaring inside my ears as I mentally chart a path from the balcony to the pediment, then a drop to the patio. It's doable. Barely.

A crow is perched on the roofline, watching me. It lifts its feathered wing and squawks as if urging me on, encouraging me to escape my gilded cage to freedom.

I hesitate. Should I wait until dark?

Probably.

But I can't be sure that I'll have access to this room again. And since Michael and one of his men are gone now, there's at least a possibility that this side of the house isn't being watched.

I nod at the crow. This is my chance, and I'm taking it.

I throw one leg over the railing, balancing my weight on the decorative stone ledge that protrudes from the house facade.

Freedom is so close.

I swing my other leg up.

And I almost make it.

A scream rips from my throat as I am yanked backward by a hand wrapping around my ankle. The crow takes flight, squawking and flapping its wings in protest.

My back slams against a hard chest, one hand clapping over my mouth while another wraps around my ribs and through my robe, his fingers painfully squeezing my breast. "*Te tango ahora.*" I've got you now.

I recognize the voice. It's the same one that said, *Let's fuck her now. No one will know, not even her.* The same one that said, *She can't scream if my dick is in her mouth.*

Anger floods my veins. Fuck. Him.

Today, I am not drugged into submission.

Today, I am not a helpless target.

Today, I am no one's victim.

The self-defense skills I learned from Burke kick in automatically. I thrust both feet forward, pushing off the railing. The man holding me staggers backward. I dig an elbow into his ribs and bite his hand at the same time.

"*Puta!*" he howls, releasing me.

But there's nowhere to go. He is standing between me

and the doorway. And a barefoot jump to the stone patio isn't an option. "Move." I issue the command like it's a foregone conclusion that he will obey me.

He doesn't.

He lunges forward just as a grin reveals yellowed teeth and a missing incisor.

This time, I am the one caught off balance. He pins me against the wall, gripping my neck and squeezing as he yanks at his belt buckle.

I can't scream. I can't breathe.

I claw at his hands with one of mine, the other digging into my pocket and for the cuticle scissor. It's not much, but it's all I've got. I jam the pointed blades between his ribs. Although they aren't long enough to inflict serious damage, he grunts in outraged surprise, loosening his grip on my neck.

I wriggle out of his hold, sucking in shallow breaths as I dart around him into the corner of the balcony. Blood is gushing from his nose, hatred blazing from his eyes. Before I can scream, he charges at me.

At the last second I duck down, sidestepping him.

Forward momentum pushes his chest over the bar but he catches himself just in time, grabbing the wrought iron with meaty paws that were intended for me, one of his feet off the ground.

I stare at his shoe for just a split second, at the scuffed sole with a tiny white pebble stuck in the black rubber tread.

This. Is. My. Chance.

I grab for his ankle, giving an upward shove with every bit of my strength.

There isn't much resistance. I have the advantage.

He cartwheels off the balcony with a loud bellow, landing on the stone patio, head first.

"Oh my God." It is a shocked rasp through trembling

fingers. What have I done?

Below me, Sebastián appears beside the body and looks up.

I've killed one of Hugo Cruz's men. It doesn't matter that he was going to rape me. It doesn't matter that I acted in self-defense. My punishment will not be determined by a judge.

The adrenaline rush that allowed me to defend myself against a man twice my size—to kill—dissipates, leaving me weak. I sink to the balcony floor, dropping my face into my hands as the tears come, shivering in my bathrobe.

I don't see the hand that grabs my hair, and I'm not at all prepared for the shocking burn of it. I cry out, simultaneously rising to my knees to relieve the pressure and flailing at the source of my pain.

"You are a curse! How many more men will die because of you?"

I'm trying to get away from the other guard, squirming and thrashing. But it's not working. His hand is a tight fist I can't escape.

And then I hear it. A quiet *click* that makes every cell in my body freeze, followed by the cold press of metal digging into my forehead.

It's almost like a thick cloud passes over the sun, or a shade spanning the globe is flipped. Instantly, everything becomes gray and colorless. Nothing else matters but the barrel pressed against my skin, the scent of fear that fills my lungs, the acrid taste of terror rising up my throat.

"Please." My heart flails inside my chest. I've made some stupid, impulsive decisions in my life … but I'm not ready for it to end. Not here. Not today.

And certainly not at the hand of someone whose first name I don't even know, whose reason for killing me isn't my fault. "You can't kill me. Not without—"

"Shut up," he spits, pulling the gun back just enough that

I'm staring straight into the barrel. "You aren't worth—"

Damon, I'm sorry I couldn't find my way back to you. I'm sorry I failed.

My apology is silent. I close my eyes, summoning the image of his face. The last thing I see will not be the gun that kills me.

If I have to die, I will descend into eternity by falling into the fierce darkness of Damon King's penetrating gaze. That blistering combination of lust and intrigue and even irritation. The piece of Damon's soul that, at least for a short time, burned for me. His warmth will carry me away.

A shot pierces the air, the grip on my hair releasing. I crumple to the ground, my head slamming into the cement paving stones.

My temple throbs. My shoulder aches. My knees burn.

But I am not dead.

chapter fifteen

Aislinn

"Fuck. We have to get out of here before the other two get back."

I stare at Sebastián's extended hand, not taking it. "You—you shot one of your father's men for me."

"I told you. I would never let any harm come to you, Aislinn. Never." Sebastián lifts me to my feet, a gun dangling from his right hand. "And right now, we have to get out of here."

I am shaking, trembling all over. But I stumble after him into the house. At some point in the last few minutes—because that's all it has been, just minutes—I've lost the belt to my robe. I don't even bother pulling the two ends together.

My mind is a hive of activity, so frenzied it's impossible to make sense of any of it. My breath is ragged and loud inside my own ears, amplified by the bass drum of my urgent heartbeat. *Go, go, go.*

We fly through the foyer and kitchen. Then a wood-paneled library that could be the same one I recently pinned to a Pinterest board and an entertaining space the size of a ballroom, skirting sofas and knocking over chairs. And finally, a cavernous mudroom that leads to a six-bay garage.

Sebastián slams a panel on the wall, raising the garage door behind a BMW. It looks like a concept car featured in commercials and car shows, one not meant for the road.

I expect it to growl when Sebastián starts the engine.

It kind of does. A loud rumble that vibrates through the leather seat beneath me. He reverses onto the white stones that had tortured the soles of my feet just an hour ago, maybe less. They spray from his tires like the wake of a speedboat when he shifts into gear and darts forward, down the long driveway.

We soar through a set of stone pillars, which is where the stone driveway becomes paved asphalt. It feels like a mile before a set of wrought-iron gates appear. Tall and imposing, each vertical black bar ends in a sharp spike that points up at the sky. Gold accents and a bold crest make the gate impressive rather than merely foreboding. And the gates are ... opening!

Relief bubbles up from the adrenaline swimming through my veins. *Go, go, go.*

And then I realize why.

The nose of a dark blue Jeep edges through them, heading our way. Even from a distance, I recognize Michael and the other man inside. "Shit," I breathe, my fingernails digging into the armrests.

Sebastián doesn't slow down or pull over.

I dare a glance at him. He is staring straight ahead, his jaw carved of granite, a vein throbbing at his temple. Both of his hands are wrapped tightly around the leather steering wheel, the knuckles of his fingers turning white.

Sebastián speeds up, keeping the car in the middle of the driveway.

He—we—are playing a game of chicken. Except it's not a game. And the death grip Sebastián has on the wheel could result in actual deaths. His. Mine. The two men in the Jeep.

But not a single ounce of me wants to shrink into my seat. I lean forward, my eyes laser-focused on the men behind the windshield of the Jeep.

Game. On. Motherfucker.

I'm mentally cheering Seb as he shifts into the highest gear, the BMW's engine a throaty purr.

Sebastián and I may have not kept in touch over the years but he is right about us leading parallel lives. We've both been pushed to the brink by forces beyond our control, and right now, we are totally in sync. We are pushing back. Hard.

The man I killed this morning—he deserved it. I'm not sorry. I feel zero remorse.

The man Sebastián killed—he deserved it, too. And from the gritted determination written on his face right now, Sebastián's not sorry about it either.

The distance between our vehicles is closing fast. Michael is hunched over the wheel, his teeth bared in a scowl.

Closer.

Closer.

Closer.

Death feels just as imminent now as it did when I had a gun pressed to my forehead.

But at the last possible second, Michael swerves into the grass. There is a metallic scrape as the side of our front bumper knocks into the opposite side of theirs, Sebastián straining to hold the wheel steady. The Jeep barrels past us and slams into a weeping Japanese maple, the trunk so wide it must have been planted a hundred years ago.

I look back, but I don't see either door opening. Sebastián makes it through the gates just as they are starting to close again.

"Oh my God." I exhale. "You did it. We're free." I sound giddy. I am giddy.

But when I look over at Sebastián, his expression is anything but happy.

"We're not free, Aislinn. We'll never be free."

I take a sobering breath. "For now, we are."

"And how long will that last?"

"What you do with your life is up to you, but I intend to stay this way."

"Los Muertos has eyes and ears everywhere. There's nowhere we can run that we won't be found."

I shake my head. "I'm not running, Seb. Not with you. And not from your father."

"And you think your father will protect you? He can't—he's just a politician with fat pockets. We'll go back to my place, figure things out together."

"No," I say emphatically. "Look at what just happened. I'm not going anywhere with you."

He gives a resigned sigh, turning onto the exit ramp of the highway and merging into traffic. "Fine. I'll drop you off at your parent's house. Lie low and have him beef up security. I'll smooth things over with my father, somehow. I'll be in touch to let you know what's going on."

"I'm not going to my parent's."

"Aislinn, I really don't think going back to your own apartment, alone, is a good idea right now."

I shudder, recalling the last time I was in my apartment. Now, there is a bedroom I'd like to set on fire. "I'm not going back there again, ever."

We aren't far from Manhattan at all. The wide green expanse of Westchester gives way to the grittier, urban Bronx. "Let me guess, you want me to bring you back to King's place?"

I give him a sleek, half-smile. "That's exactly what I

want."

chapter sixteen

Damon

Burke screeches to a stop halfway down a long driveway. "What the fuck?"

Once we began diving deeper into Sebastián Cruz's client list, we created a list of potential locations he might have taken Aislinn. This Bronxville estate was one of several that peaked our interest.

I just hope it's not too late.

We both jump out, running toward the still smoking carcass of a Jeep whose crumpled hood now looks like an accordion, courtesy of a squat maple tree surrounded by mulch and several smaller plants.

I head for the already opened front driver-side door, discovering only an empty seat.

On the other side, Burke has the passenger door open and is pressing his fingers against the neck of the man whose head is bent at an unnatural angle, confirming the obvious. "He's gone."

We jog back to our car and head toward the house, filling Finley in as we go. "Teams two and three are just behind you, pulling in now," she says.

This time, our guns are already drawn when we get out of the car. The other teams arrive as I'm walking up the front. Burke directs them to fan out around the house and he takes my back. I'm through the front door when Team Two discovers a second dead body on the back patio.

Fuck. This isn't good. My steps are heavy, weighed down with dread at what I might find around each corner.

Team Three finds another body on a second-floor terrace.

What we don't find is Aislinn Granville.

Finley's voice comes through my earpiece. "Picking up chatter about a Los Muertos clean-up crew needed up north. I think you should get out of there."

"There's gotta be something we're missing. I can feel it." And I can. "Aislinn was here, I'm sure of it."

I'm standing in one of the bedrooms, running agitated hands through my hair when I notice the wet towels slung over the shower.

Except that, on closer examination, they're not towels at all. They're Aislinn's clothes. Her black skirt. Her bra and panties. Her blouse.

Her *bloodstained* blouse.

The roar that explodes from the deepest part of my belly is guttural, that of a savage beast. My fist pounds the frameless glass door, shattering it into a million pieces. They fall at my feet, glistening like confetti.

Burke takes Aislinn's shirt from my left hand and wraps it around the bloody knuckles of my right. "Come on, boss."

"She was fucking here." I seethe. Just like in the basement of the chapel, where I found long blonde hairs clinging to a dirty, child-sized mattress shoved into a fucking closet.

My body is not big enough to contain the rage swelling inside every cell of my body. My veins are bursting with it, my bones are aching from it, my vision is tainted from it.

I. Am. Rage.

A filthy stream of vitriol explodes from my mouth as I stomp down the stairs. Orders mixed with profanity mixed with angry threats.

Finley tries several times to interrupt, but I talk over her, unwilling to accept even a single excuse. Finally, a shrill burst of noise shocks me into shutting up. "What the—"

"Check out the security camera feed, right fucking now."

chapter seventeen

Aislinn

*D*amon's apartment is empty.

Really empty.

I wander through the rooms, finding not a single guard. Not even Mrs. Weathersby. I'm back in the foyer when Finley bursts through the elevator doors. She stops short when she sees me.

For a moment, neither of us says anything. The doors close again, leaving us wrapped in silence so thick I can hear the rush of air through the vents as the car descends back to the lobby.

I pull my bathrobe more tightly around me, shifting on my bare feet. "Are you o—" Finley stops short of saying *okay* and instead asks, "Can I do anything to help you?"

I shake my head. "No, I'm fine." My reply is automatic. I'm not hurt, but I'm definitely not *fine*.

Finley merely blinks. "Damon's on his way back. He should be here in less than half an hour."

Half an hour. It feels like a long, long time. "Where is he?"

"He was at the estate in Westchester, looking for you."

"Oh." I stumble backward a few steps, sinking into the narrow bench set against the wall facing the elevator. "He must have gotten there just after we left."

A minute passes, maybe more. The silence is awkward and yet not. The past four days have been so emotionally charged, now that I'm back in the cocoon of Damon's apartment, my mind is foggy. "He's been looking for me, all this time?"

"He has," she says with a nod. "We all have."

Some of the fog clears and I remember what Sebastián said. *King's about to be dethroned.*

I regard Finley with fresh eyes and a suspicious heart. What if she's the mole?

I'm not comfortable being alone with her right now. "Does Damon know I'm back? Is he on his way here?"

Another nod. "Yes. I was on the line with him when you walked into the lobby downstairs."

More silence. This time Finley breaks it. "Do you want to talk, to tell me what happened?"

She's not asking in a shady way, but … "No," I answer, rising to my feet. "I think I'm going to wait in Damon's bedroom."

Finley frowns, although she doesn't make any move to stop me. Passing her, every hair on my body stands on end, goose bumps racing across my flesh. I expect her to grab me, or to hear the sound of a cocked gun.

Whether it's shades of PTSD or just gut instinct, I can barely breathe as I walk down the hall. By the time I reach Damon's door and throw myself behind it, I'm wheezing and gasping for air.

I don't bother attempting to lock it. All security is controlled electronically; if Finley wants to get inside, I can't stop her.

I walk to the window, the one that overlooks the front entrance.

And I wait for my dark knight to storm his castle.

chapter eighteen

Damon

The tinted glass of the elevator reflects a man who looks like me—dark eyes, sharp jaw, slightly unruly black hair.

But inside, I sure as fuck don't feel like me.

I've changed. Or, rather, Aislinn Granville has changed me. I dragged her into my world, a place where crime and corruption are the norm. Where brutality and vengeance are standard operating procedure. Where emotions don't exist.

I told myself Aislinn was an indulgent reward I'd earned by maintaining the balance of power in my city. Merely a temporary diversion, a harmless vice. Surely her lips couldn't be as sweet, her skin as soft, her hair as silky smooth as it appeared from afar. Surely her voice would grate on my ears, her scent would irritate my throat, her resistance would cease to amuse.

But none of that happened.

Instead, I allowed the balance of power to shift, away from me. I lost control. Of myself, of my enemies, of my city. I turned Aislinn into a useful pawn. A chess piece to be played.

What is a king if he can't protect his queen?

I lied—to myself. Over and over and over. Lies that have been choking me from the moment she was taken.

If Aislinn was a temporary diversion, a harmless vice, an indulgent reward—she would have been expendable. Collateral damage of a brutal but necessary war.

She is none of those things.

How can someone be temporary when they're etched into my bones? How can someone be expendable if I've killed, over and over, to get them back?

Aislinn Granville is everything to me.

Every. Fucking. Thing.

Finley is waiting for me when I step into the hall. She points wordlessly toward my bedroom.

I take a moment to gather my thoughts before opening the door. But it's unnecessary. All my thoughts are of Aislinn Granville. She is the air I breathe. The beat of my heart. The light to my dark. The goddess of my dreams.

"Aislinn." Her name is a relieved exhale, a whispered word of thanks.

She spins away from the window when I open the door, and my vision is immediately filled with a halo of wavy blonde hair, honeyed skin, and eyes as deep and blue as the ocean.

Twin tides of relief and shame batter me as I cross the room and wrap my arms around Aislinn's narrow waist, cradling her against me. Her weight is negligible, but I've never held anything more valuable. "You're back."

Small hands close around my shoulders, her chest a pillowy press against mine. I feel the flutter of her eyelashes against my neck, the warm wetness of a tear sliding down my skin.

"It's so good to be home," she whispers.

Home. The word hits me like the bolt of a Taser, the sharp sizzle a powerful jolt dead in the center of my chest. Because I know Aislinn didn't mean this building or my apartment. She means me. *I* am her home.

And she is mine.

I don't deserve her. I didn't keep her safe from Los Muertos.

I didn't save her.

But letting go of Aislinn isn't even a thought in my mind as I carry her through my apartment. And by the way she is clinging to me, it is clear the feeling is entirely mutual. Each breath is infused with her honeyed scent, my lungs buzzing from intoxication.

A part of me has been closed off, fused completely shut, for so long. But with Aislinn, that place is practically wide open, bared to her. Whatever boundaries I once had have been breached. Rules I'd enacted years ago have been rendered null and void.

When the tightness clutching at my throat loosens, I ask, "How did you get back here?"

"That's not important," she says emphatically. "We need to talk. You're in danger."

Aislinn must take my incredulous stare for fear, because she rushes to explain. "Cruz has infiltrated your organization. As soon as he has access to your accounts—" she breaks off as tears fill her eyes.

My heart thumps erratically inside my chest, pulsing with the strangest sensation. Utter bewilderment. "You came back here … to warn me?"

I know the answer to my question before she bobs her head.

Of course, she did. Only Aislinn Granville would feel the need to protect her monster.

I sigh, drawing her back into my arms. "And you heard all this from Sebastián Cruz, correct?"

She offers a reluctant nod.

"I'm hardly inclined to believe a word he says." But I'm very fucking inclined to beat the crap out of him for planting ideas in Aislinn's head she shouldn't be worrying about.

"I really think—"

I press a finger to Aislinn's lips. "But I will look into it." I have a small, but extremely well-vetted staff. It won't take long. My recent doubts about Finley were more about me than her, and resolving them took minutes.

Once I feel the tension in her shoulders ease a bit, I say, "Tell me everything, from the beginning."

She hesitates, her breath catching. "Can't it just be *us* for a little while longer?"

I shift Aislinn so that she's looking directly at my face and I into hers. Taking time to ourselves is an almost irresistible indulgence. "Princess ..."

She blinks up at me, her bright gaze swirling with understanding, the pink pout of her lips conveying hope. "I'm here now, with you. We're together. We're safe. I've told you about what I heard."

"Yes, and I'm not worried about it. I'm worried about you."

"Don't be. I'm here with you, exactly where I want to be. Exactly where I belong."

I groan as a fresh wave of guilt surges, clutching at my ribs and compressing my lungs. I loosen my hold, letting Aislinn slide down my body until she's standing on her feet in front of me. A moment passes as we merely stare at each other, feasting with our eyes. Aislinn's pupils dilate with desire, the blue of her irises glowing like the hottest part of a flame.

"I want to know everything that's happened to you in the last four days."

Her cheeks flush. "Are you saying that your needs trump

mine?"

I bite back an exasperated sigh. "And what are your needs?"

She pokes a finger in my chest. "You, damn it."

Jesus Fucking Christ.

This girl.

She slays me, tapping into my most animalistic possessiveness. The deep-seated need to claim—reclaim— what is mine. What's always been mine. With Aislinn, those games of dominance and submission I've played in the past feel unnecessary. My need to dominate, her willingness to submit, they are etched into the fabric of our souls and go beyond sexual scenes. She appeals to me at a cellular level, satisfying my needs without arbitrary expectations and rules.

I take a deep breath and cinch my hands at Aislinn's waist, pulling her back against me.

Aislinn Granville is a beautiful blonde wrecking ball— laying waste to everything I thought I needed, everything I thought I knew.

All that I'd once believed to be true.

Right now ... all I need is Aislinn. All I know is Aislinn.

She is my truth.

The lies I've told her, the truths I've held back—they pollute the breaths I take, coating my tongue with bitterness. There is so much I should share. So much I will share. But not right now.

Not right now, when Aislinn's heart is beating so rapidly against mine.

Not right now, when her fingers are entwined at the back of my neck, her forehead pressed into the hollow between my jaw and shoulder.

Not right now, when she is making this needy sound, trapped somewhere between a whine and a whimper, that has my dick swelling and pulsing, every step a twinge of discomfort clutching at my balls.

I thought I was a strong man. Invincible and invulnerable. Physically. Financially. Mentally. Emotionally.

The woman in my arms has taken that away from me even as she's proved it true.

Right now, my knees are weak with this wanting, needing, must-fucking-having.

Because right now, there is no distinction between need and want, necessity and luxury.

Aislinn Granville is both. And I want, need, must-fucking-have her.

Right here. Right now.

chapter nineteen

Aislinn

My heartbeat is an erratic, distracting pitter-patter against my ribs as I take in the stark beauty of the man standing in front of me. He looks like the same man I ran from just days ago. Almost.

The same rich black hair and inky eyelashes. The same strong, shadowed jawline and high, elegant cheekbones. The same spark of intensity lighting up those dark, dark eyes.

But there are smudges beneath them. And faint horizontal lines, like the silvery remnants of a shattered spider web, cross his forehead.

Damon is glaring at me like an adversary he's torn between spanking or fucking. There is yearning in his gaze, a faint glimmer of tenderness beneath his infuriated expression.

I like it. A lot.

The panic and fear and pure terror that filled my veins just a few hours ago hasn't yet evaporated. Those intense emotions are still there, like toxins that have yet to be flushed from my system. I don't want to be treated with kid gloves.

Not by Damon King.

I need his intensity now more than ever. I am desperate to revel in the raging storm Damon and I create when we're together. The kind of storm that deserves a name. Deserves to be written in history books for its power ... and for the toll of its destruction.

I want the shocking illumination of lightning. The ominous energy of thunder.

I want to give and take.

Clash and break.

Writhe and shake.

"Damon," I say his name like a warning. *I need the man—the monster—who claimed me as his own. My savage king.*

He presses a firm kiss to my forehead, his fingers lightly pushing into the hair at the base of my scalp. "Tell me this," he says. "Is there any hurt I can't kiss better?"

The throaty rumble of Damon's voice is like a liberal pour of molasses on my frayed nerves. "No." My nose is flush with his chest and I breathe deep that scent I didn't think I would ever smell again. Wood and whiskey and raw masculinity. So damn intoxicating.

He sweeps his tongue along the rim of my ear. "Is there any hurt I can't lick better?"

The tension in my shoulders eases as I flatten my palms against his chest. "No."

Damon lifts my chin, our eyes locking on each other. "Is there any hurt I can't fuck better?"

My cheeks warm as I draw my lower lip between my teeth. Then I shake my head slowly. "No."

He smiles that darkly seductive grin and my stomach flips. "Let's go take a shower."

I nod my head eagerly. A long hot shower sounds perfect. A long hot shower—with my savage king—sounds downright exquisite. By the time the water is running, my borrowed bathrobe is just a white smudge of bad memory strewn across the tile floor.

Damon begins unbuttoning his shirt and I eagerly reach for his belt. When he is as naked as I am, he cups my chin between his thumb and forefinger and tips it upward. His kiss is hard but not punishing. The perfect amount of pressure.

I moan low in my throat.

He growls in return. And when we pull apart, we are wearing matching lust-drunk grins.

"Do you trust me?" he asks.

"I thought you said I shouldn't trust anyone who has to ask."

"I'm asking now."

The truth falls from my lips. "With my life."

He pulls me into the shower with a leer on his face, his voice a gritted rasp of desire. "How about with your ass?"

My response is a nervous, high-pitched giggle that dies in my throat when I realize Damon isn't teasing me. His question is real. Do I trust him to do … *that*? I swallow, ducking my head as a heated flush surges above my collarbone, burning the tips of my ears. My whisper evaporates into the cloud of mist rising around us. "Yes."

chapter twenty

Damon

$\mathcal{R}$elief has invaded the marrow of my bones. I am filled with it. Overflowing with it.

Whether it's male pride or misplaced possessiveness or something else entirely ... I am simply grateful for the tragedy Aislinn has not born.

No one has stolen what is only hers to give.

A gift she's given to me. A gift she's about to give to me again.

All that matters to me at this moment is her cobalt stare shining with trust, the scent of honey filling my lungs with every breath, the velvety smoothness of her skin beneath my fingertips.

Aislinn Granville is my gift from a god I stopped believing in years ago. An angel bestowed to a devil.

I'll take her. I'll treasure her. I'll live for her. I'll die for her.

And I'll commit all seven sins—countless times, with zero regrets—to keep her.

I want to kiss her, consume her, taste and touch and

explore every inch of her. I want to fuck her everywhere, in every way. I want to be her first, her last, her everything. I want to be hers.

I am hers.

Aislinn's cheek is pressed to my chest, water coming at us from every angle. I inhale a deep breath of the warm mist, my hands wrapping around Aislinn's narrow waist, my fingertips resting along the hollowed dimples that sit just below the base of her spine. Water droplets slide and scurry over her silken skin.

My dick is so hard it throbs. But I'm more aware of this feeling of completeness, of contentment, sitting heavily inside my chest. Heavy, but not weighted. Despite all that has happened, all that still needs to happen, in this moist enclosure, holding Aislinn against my body—I feel lighter than I have since ...

Since ever.

Just then, Aislinn lifts her head, her wet hair sliding against my chest. "I can hear you."

My brows draw together. "I didn't say anything."

"You did, actually. You let out this deep sigh, and when you squeezed me, you moaned."

"I moaned?" I'd been so lost in my own thoughts, I hadn't realized any of that.

She laughs. "It was a good moan. A happy moan."

"I didn't realize moans could be interpreted."

"Everything can be interpreted. And that sigh, that moan," her spiky eyelashes flutter, "it said, you're happy I'm back."

I pause for a moment, unused to putting my feelings into words. "Yeah, princess. I'm really fucking happy you're home. I was losing my goddamn mind." There's so much more I want to say. That I don't know if I will ever recover from losing her, even temporarily. That I will carry the shame of it forever. That I don't deserve her.

But my feelings are too big for words. I slide my hands up her sides, over her shoulders, cupping my palms over her cheeks, my thumbs sweeping a mix of tears and water from beneath her eyes.

Fuck, she's beautiful.

The kind of beautiful that goes beyond what can be seen on the surface. The canvas created by skin as luminous as mother-of-pearl, the long limbs and lush curves and loose tumble of hair that captures every shade of blonde from platinum to gold to bronze. Azure blue eyes, plump pink lips, startlingly black lashes.

Yes, Aislinn Granville is a beauty.

But my spitfire is so much more than that.

"Good," she says simply.

I reach for the feminine bottles of soap and shampoo and conditioner that line the ledge of my shower, alongside my own. I lather, rinse, and repeat until Aislinn shines like a new penny. I rub and massage until her shoulders are loose and her head is heavy on her graceful neck.

I am about to shut off the water when Aislinn stills my hand. "Your turn."

She pours shampoo in her hands, motioning for me to turn around.

Instead, I drop to my knees at her feet and lean my head back. Aislinn's breasts swing over my face as her fingers push into my hair, her nails scratching my scalp. A groan slips past my lips just before I take one of Aislinn's breasts into my mouth. My balls swell and harden from the pure pleasure of Aislinn's hands in my hair, the sweet clean taste of her in my mouth, the needy furl of her nipple pressing against my tongue.

I cup a breast in one hand, sliding my other between her thighs. A shiver trembles through Aislinn's body at my touch. I part her slit with one finger, dragging the tip through her seam that splits open so readily for me. Pride swells inside my chest at the wetness leaking out from between her folds. Wetness that has nothing to do with the spray of the shower and everything to do with me. I do this to her.

A needy whine falls from her mouth as I add another finger, going deeper this time. Her hips buck forward as I slide over her clit.

Shifting my position, I take her other breast into my mouth. As I knew it would, this one tastes just as sweet, her nipple even harder and firmer after my teasing and pinching.

After Aislinn rinses the suds from my hair, I back her up against the wall of the shower by moving forward on my knees. I pull away from her breast and look up. Her nipples are a rich ruby, startling against her skin like wine spilled on a snow-white tablecloth. Droplets of water cling to her curves, sparkling like diamonds.

"Please, Damon," she says. "I stayed strong, but right now, I just need to fall apart in your arms." Trust and lust and a blissful kind of elation are smeared across Aislinn's face like a thin film of Vaseline on a lens. Clear but obvious.

Only a sliver of blue clinging to the dilated vortex of Aislinn's pupils glints at me. A blue that is so bright, so blinding, it flays the skin from my body. I'm a skeleton barely held together by a knotted network of exposed nerves and vulnerable muscles.

I am an unguarded fortress.

My gates are open, my weapons surrendered. All for this woman. For my spitfire with the power to incinerate me.

And maybe she will, but not until I set her on fire.

"You're not going to fall today, princess. In my arms, you'll soar."

I hook one of her legs over my shoulder, then the other. Until her pussy is right where it belongs, in front of my face.

Our eyes are still locked when I open my mouth and extend my tongue, giving her a long lick. "Jesus," Aislinn mutters, her head falling back against the marble as her hands plunge into my hair, twisting the wet strands within her grip.

I am lost to the intoxicating taste of her. A sharp sweetness just barely distilled by an exotic earthiness. My tongue darts and dives, lapping and licking. My hands are curved around her ass and I can't help but squeeze the warm, wet flesh in my fingers. Her thighs are firm around my neck, the heels of her feet tapping out a desperate rhythm as they beat against my back.

I am in fucking heaven.

Literally. Aislinn's cunt is the most delicious I've ever tasted, her skin is the softest, her moans and groans and squeals and sighs are a symphony I will never tire of.

Her pussy is my paradise.

I am so eager, so ravenous, so goddamn *hungry*. Aislinn's fingers twitch, her nails scraping my scalp as they tug on my hair, her thighs shaking against my jaw as she comes with a gasping cry, her back arching, hips bucking.

After several long moments, she relaxes her grip on my hair, the fluttering contractions of her internal muscles finally ceasing as her thighs go slack and a final, deep sigh leaves her lungs. I lift my head, feeling her wetness spread all over my lips and chin and jaw.

Aislinn looks down at me and gives a shaky laugh, wiping at my face with one of her hands. "You really made a meal of me, huh?"

I bite her inner thigh, hard enough for her to squeak. "That was just the first course."

chapter twenty-one

Aislinn

My legs are wobbly when Damon sets me down. His strong hands wrap around my waist, holding me steady. A rush of gratitude comes over me. I stare up at him and smile, knowing I am also grateful for his full lips and wide mouth and his sinful, skillful tongue.

I'm grateful for him.

I'm grateful to be here.

I'm grateful to be alive.

He presses a kiss to my forehead and brings us both back under the water for a moment. I close my eyes as it cascades over my head, streaking down my face, my shoulders, my back. It feels so good.

And then Damon adjusts a dial and the various streams and sprays become more of a warm, gentle mist. Like a wet sauna. He slicks his hair back from his head and I watch the interplay of biceps and triceps in his arms. There's an innate efficiency and grace to his movements. Damon reminds me of a big game cat. A cheetah or panther, all sleek muscles and dark, devious eyes.

An animal that enjoys playing with his prey before going in for the kill.

And he definitely knows how to play.

I bite at my lower lip, the endorphin rush from my orgasm dissolving from an onslaught of nerves. "What's next?"

The grin that lifts Damon's cheeks sends my stomach plummeting just before he lowers his head and captures my mouth with his own. I moan, a fresh surge of desire flowing through my veins. There's something unabashedly carnal about tasting myself on his tongue.

"I'm glad you asked. But it's better if I show you." His lips hover over my mouth, each syllable a soft, breathy kiss. "And just remember that you trust me, okay, spitfire?"

"Mm-hmm." My hands curl around the base of his neck, wishing I could stop time. Wishing we could stay frozen in this moment, exchanging steamy kisses. Our naked bodies pressed against each other, a tangle of slippery skin and hungry mouths, grasping hands and needy moans.

But Damon ends our kiss, nipping along the line of my jaw before sucking the fleshy lobe of my ear into his mouth. A delicious shiver cartwheels down my spine.

"Turn around and lean forward, hands against the tile."

My shiver becomes a tremble as I pull away to look at his face, then at the thick shaft jutting from his body. It points at me like an accusation. "I'm not sure about this, Damon."

"Are you sure of me?" His voice is deep and gruff, and I am sure that if I said *no*, he would grab a towel and this would all be over.

But that would be a lie. I am one hundred percent certain of the man standing in front of me. He may be a panther, but I am not his prey.

I don't answer right away. Instead, I do as instructed. I pivot slowly. Bending at my hips and stretching my arms out, pressing my palms against the marble. And when I look over my shoulder at Damon, I finally say, "Sure enough to light a fire in a locked room."

His lips twitch in response, then open to release a full-throated laugh that wraps around my ribs like the warmest of embraces. His fingers trace the curve of my spine. "Only you, Aislinn Granville. Only you."

His words slay me while his hands work their magic. Dipping lower, into the crack of my ass, hesitating over the fluttering hole before continuing to my still drenched folds. He enters me, thrusting deep. I close my eyes in bliss, my head dropping forward from my neck like a forgotten puppet.

Because the puppet master is occupied with what's between my legs. I gulp at humid air; the steam impeding my ability to extract oxygen from it. My head is spinning, but all that matters is Damon's hand, Damon's touch. His fingers alternate between sliding in and sliding over my still swollen, sensitive clit.

A pour of ... *something*, could be oil or lotion or lube or even conditioner, I'm too busy chasing another orgasm to care, lands on the base of my spine and then flows into the crack between my ass cheeks. It's just another layer of sensation. I know what's coming; I do. But pleasure is a solid dam against the nervous anticipation.

A finger breaches my tight outer ring. The feeling is foreign, but not unpleasant. There is no pain. I arch my spine, pushing back against him. A second finger steals my breath, and instead of pain, there is only more pleasure. *Ohmygod.* It's a barely there whisper. A shocked admission.

Damon's low chuckle is proof that he heard. "I'm going to make this good for you. Keep trusting me, princess."

"Okay," I choke out, the word becoming a high-pitched wheeze when I feel Damon add a third finger. Instead of straining toward him, my body instinctively bucks away.

"Breathe," he urges, curving the fingers inside my pussy to rub at my inner wall.

I don't breathe. I can't. My climax breaks over me, shards of ecstasy raining down over my arched back, my upturned head, my shaking ass. Two of my holes are filled when my mouth opens. A surprised cry escapes, the sound reverberating through the glass enclosure, ringing through the air.

Damon's hands move to my hips as he guides his cock through my slit, piercing me deep. He rides me while my pussy clenches and quivers, his thrusts drawing out my orgasm as my hands slide down the marble wall until they are flat against the ledge. I am practically a triangle now, and I hear Damon groan as he squeezes my ass cheeks then pulls them apart. I know what he's looking at. Know that he's about to claim this last vestige of virgin territory.

Suddenly, I want it so badly. I want to feel Damon in my darkest, tightest place. To be claimed by this man. It is his; I am his.

Damon leans down, folding his chest over my back, his cock still inside me. "How're you doing, spitfire?"

"Make me yours, Damon," I breathe. And I mean it.

He plants a kiss on my shoulder blade, his hands sliding beneath my arms to cup my breasts, his fingers toying with my nipples. I moan, swiveling my hips and pushing back against him.

Slowly, almost leisurely, Damon straightens. His hands slide along the frets of my ribs, curving in at my waist until they settle over my hip bones. He pulls out, all the way to the tip before slamming back inside me, the crown of his cock kissing my womb once, twice, three times. A whorl of sensation envelops me, the tentative stirrings of another orgasm clutching at my belly.

But the next time he pulls out, there's no corresponding

forward thrust. Instead, I feel his dick sliding down, the crown teasing my clit. "Holy shit," I gasp. It's thick and hot, gliding over my most sensitive nerve endings. I am mindless with lust, an insect caught in the web of its own desire. I could come from this, so hard. Just the press of his cock against my clit, this ruthless rubbing.

My arms are shaking when he pulls away, dragging his length through my weeping slit. By the time I feel his thickness pressing against my quivering entrance, I would get down on my knees and beg for it, except that that would put me in the entirely wrong position.

So I rise up on the balls of my feet, trying to communicate how much I want this, need this. Now.

My body belongs to this beautiful beast.

Take me. Take all of me. Now, now, now.

I'm at the deep end of the ocean, staring into the abyss. *Push me in, Damon.*

"Breathe, Aislinn," he says again. This time I listen. I open my mouth to inhale, just as he begins to push forward.

I can feel my muscles being stretched, pushed apart. And at first, it feels good. Like the most delicious kind of pressure.

Until it doesn't. Until the pressure stops being pleasure and becomes pain. Like I'm being cut, or burned, or both.

Suddenly, I'm sucking in air through gritted teeth, trying not to cry out. All those feel-good endorphins have crashed into a brick wall and hit the ground. And I crash too. I'm only being held upright by the strength of Damon's hands at my hips, by the part of him invading a part of me that's not meant to accommodate. "Fight through, spitfire," Damon grits out, and I want to cry. Because I want to give this part of myself to him so badly.

But I don't think I can.

Somehow he manages to adjust the shower settings again, and some of the lower jets begin emitting more than just a warm spray of mist. One of them in particular hits right between my legs just as Damon pushes past the last of my resistance, his flared tip finally notched inside of me. "The hard part is over. Don't worry, I keep my promises."

He already is. The water pressure is just strong enough, and just at the perfect place, to send a shiver of memory through me. A tingling reminder of the pleasure from just a few minutes ago.

Instinct takes over. My hands push against the ledge, my back hollows out, my hips squirm and buck, trying to take more of Damon's cock. And then this feeling of fullness, of wrongness, of being stretched too much ... doesn't feel bad at all. I want more of it, more of Damon. Deeper, harder.

That jet of water is magic. And there's something unexpectedly erotic about having Damon's cock in my ass.

"Fuck, Aislinn. You feel so fucking good."

Ditto. The word is in my head, but what comes out is a garbled, unintelligible moan of surprise. Of wonder. And as Damon slowly slides all the way in, so deep that I can feel his balls pressed up tight against my pussy, even of pleasure.

He drops kisses on my shoulder blades, bites down on the curve between my neck and my shoulder. "You're the most perfect dream."

Surrounded by a cloud of mist, it feels like we are in a dream. Like the events of the past few days never actually happened.

We are living in a fantasy, and I never want to wake up.

Damon pulls out until barely the tip remains before driving back in, slow and steady. His hands pry my cheeks apart and I can feel the singe of his stare as he watches his thickness invading my tiny virgin hole.

Even though the water pressure of the spray aimed at my clit hasn't increased, the intensity of it has. I try to squirm away, but Damon doesn't let me. The pleasure of it, the pleasure of Damon entering me in a place where no one else ever has, they slice at me like the sharpest of blades.

Shredding me completely.

I am in tatters as Damon continues his relentless assault. Wrecked and ruined.

Ecstasy is so close, a shimmering snow globe I can't find a way into.

"Please, please." I'm knocking on the glass sphere, not even sure what I'm asking for. Faster, harder, deeper. More.

Just ... more.

More of this. More of him. More of us.

Just, *more*.

As if he hears me, Damon slides a hand over my hip and between my thighs. Cupping my heat. Blocking the spray. I am grateful. I can focus entirely on how he feels inside me, in that strange and unexpected place.

I have never felt so full, so overwhelmed, so *worshipped*, as he drives himself inside me with long, powerful strokes. Nerve endings I never knew I had stand up and wave, cheering at this new experience.

Pure, rolling waves of pleasure penetrate me. An ocean of it, undulating and effervescent. And I dive in.

Behind me, Damon is grunting each time he slams into me, his thighs slapping my ass, one hand gripping my hip while the other is pressed against my pussy.

We are sprinters, our breaths coming in ragged pants as we race toward the finish line. There is a desperate flutter in the pit of my stomach, a definite clench and twist.

"Come for me now, princess," Damon rasps, removing the shield of his hand so that the water hits my clit at the same time as he bottoms out deep inside me.

My third climax comes at me like a riptide, surging over my head and pulling me deep into the undertow. I cry out as I break apart, caught between the precise aim of a water jet in front of me and the perfection that is Damon's cock drilling into me from behind. I can't see. I can't catch my breath. My arms are trembling so hard they are barely supporting me. It is Damon holding me in place. I feel completely out of control.

His deep bellow merges with the final notes of my own cry. Damon fucks his way through his own climax and I can feel him pulsing inside my ass, filling me in a place that has never been filled before.

And for a long moment, Damon folds himself over my back, his warm breath blowing chills over the naked knobs of my spine, his big hands wrapping around my waist, crisscrossing so that my breasts are captured by his palms.

Our heart rates slow, our breaths easing. We are at peace.

But it doesn't last. It can't. Damon pulls out of me slowly, then gently eases me into an upright position. I turn to face him and for a moment all we do is stare at each other, blinking in the moist air. Something has changed between us—and not just because of a sex act.

I slip back into Damon's arms and he washes me again, adjusting the controls so that the spray returns to full strength and carries the suds down the drain.

After wrapping me in a plush towel, he kisses the top of my head and swings me into his arms. "I hope you're not too tired. There's a lot we have to talk about."

Reality rushes in. Yes, there is so much I need to tell him.

But I am still clinging to that perfect, peaceful moment. The warm, safe haven of Damon's embrace.

Talk of Los Muertos and Sebastián and my father will destroy it.

I'm terrified it will destroy us too.

chapter twenty two

Damon

By the time I turn off the water and cover Aislinn with an oversized bath towel, she is a slippery, loose-limbed doll. As she wobbles on her feet, I reach beneath her knees and back, sweeping her into my arms.

With my lust sated, at least temporarily, my need for vengeance has returned to the forefront of my mind. I tuck Aislinn beneath the sheets and slide beside her.

This will likely be the most gentle interrogation I've ever conducted—it is certainly the only one I've ever conducted naked. But there is so much I need to know.

"So," I begin, settling Aislinn so that her cheek is resting on my chest as I lean back against the headboard.

She releases a sigh, her eyelashes fluttering over my pectoral muscles. "So," she echoes.

"How did you get away?" It's not the question I meant to ask. I intended to have Aislinn start from the very beginning. From the moment she stepped out onto the street.

"Ah, well … after I killed one of Cruz's men—"

I am shocked, stunned, my blood turning to ice at her

hesitant explanation.

Aislinn isn't like me. She wouldn't hurt anyone unless she was provoked. "You *killed* … Wait … What the fuck did he do to you?" Bile climbs up my throat as I look at Aislinn's body, recalling what *I'd* done to her. I am a fucking animal. What was I thinking? I should have—

"Hey." Aislinn rises up on her elbow, a hand moving to my shoulder, shaking me. "Damon, stop. Please. Look at me."

My unfocused eyes find her face, blinking until her elegant contours and symmetrical lines are clear once again. "Spitfire. Did I hurt you?"

"Of course not." She lays her sweet pink lips on mine, the warmth of her breath ghosting over my mouth an instant before her soft kiss. "You have never done anything to me I haven't wanted and wouldn't have begged for."

"But I—"

"Those self-defense moves came in handy." Her forehead is still pressed to mine. "I'm okay, really. And Sebastián brought me back to you."

The churning anger inside my gut returns to a full boil. "He's why you were there."

"No. Hugo Cruz is why I was there. Sebastián is no more a cartel soldier than I am a corrupt politician. He and I are both—"

"You're what? A team now?"

She pulls back, tilting her head to the side. "Damon, I'm here with you. You and I, we're the team. That's what I'm trying to tell you. I'm on your side."

"Why?" The question slips out of my mouth like a nervous tic. It might be the only question that matters.

She sighs, looking at me from beneath lowered lashes as the corners of her lips curl slowly upward. "Because there's nowhere else I'd rather be."

I cup my hands around Aislinn's face, my thumbs resting in the hollow between her cheekbone and jaw. "That makes two of us." I kiss the worried frown etched into her forehead, the pert slope of her nose, the pink pout of her lips. "But you're still not off the hook."

Silence stretches out as she worries at her lower lip.

I wait, knowing it is often the most effective tactic to gain useful information.

It works. After a few minutes Aislinn begins speaking, her words raining down on me like shrapnel.

Drugged.

Duct taped to a chair.

Threatened.

Slapped.

It takes every ounce of restraint I possess to remain calm. To listen, pressing light kisses against Aislinn's forehead as I stroke her neck and back and arms and shoulders. All the parts of her that I can reach, using soft soothing touches as her words explode inside my ears.

"I-I think they were talking about you. At first, I wasn't sure. *El rey corrupto.* The corrupt king. After what you said about my father, I thought maybe they were talking about him. But that's not true—they were talking about you, weren't they?"

I nod. "Yes. That's what I'm called."

"Why?" Her forehead nuzzles into my neck. "What exactly do you do, Damon?"

"You don't know?" After all these years, I'm well aware that my reputation precedes me. I would think Aislinn knows exactly the nature of my business.

"I've heard rumors and innuendos. Suspicions. But, no. And there's no need for me to distinguish fact from fiction if you're perfectly capable of telling me the truth."

"I probably shouldn't."

"I'm a part of this now, a part of you. I need to know," she whispers.

I want to argue. Insist that Aislinn is in no way a part of *this*, even though there's no denying she's a part of *me*. The darkness I thrive in, the corruption I control. The bribes and scheming in back alleys and boardrooms, the evil that exists below paved streets and priceless real estate.

New York is a glamorous city surrounded by a toxic river. Our dazzling skyline is a distraction from what lurks beneath the murky, polluted water.

Aislinn Granville belongs to that world. The glamorous one. She deserves to wear evening gowns at exclusive charity events, champagne in her hand and stilettos on her feet.

Except that right now, she's here with me. And if I'm unwilling to give her up—she is right. I have to let her in. I have to explain the gritty slice of New York's underworld that I control. This purgatory that serves felons and politicians, crime bosses and bureaucrats.

She shifts against my chest, sensing the disquiet rushing through my veins. "How ... How did a little kid that wanted to save the world become—"

"—me?" I interrupt before she says something I won't be able to unhear. Only from Aislinn do I crave approval. "I went to prison. And that was where everything changed. My cellmate ran an entire criminal organization from behind bars. He'd been doing it for years, but it was getting harder. At first, I wasn't interested, but ..." My voice trails off as I remember that time in my life.

Aislinn is right there with me. "But then your mother died," she prompts.

"Right. And that was when I lost interest in ever fitting back into society again. One thing led to another and when I was released, Ace asked me to—" My jaw snaps shut when Aislinn jerks upright. *Fuck.*

"Ace," she repeats, daggers of accusation glinting at me from her wide eyes. "The man my mother mentioned. The man you denied knowing anything about."

"Aislinn," I groan. "It's not my story to tell."

"There's a *story*?" She says the word like a curse.

I run a hand through my hair, pulling at the ends. "You should really ask your mother about him."

She sits up, wrapping the covers around her chest. "I did, remember? You were there. She wouldn't, or couldn't, tell me. And according to Chad—"

A scowl automatically pulls at my lips. "When did you talk to Chad about Ace?"

"That night. After we left my mother's house and I went to the office."

"Because you said you forgot something. Was that—"

"Oh, no." A pointed fingernail pushes into my chest. "Don't try to change the subject. I asked Chad if the name meant anything to him, and he said the only Ace he knew of was a former crime boss who was either still in jail or dead. Which is it? Is he still in jail?"

I glare at her for a beat before deciding to concede the point. "No. He's gone."

To my surprise, Aislinn doesn't look any less angry at my admission. A flush has risen up her chest, her clavicle glowing almost pink below her pale neck. "Gone? Or dead?"

"He was granted compassionate release. I was with him when he died." I pause. "And so was your mother."

"My mother?" The suspicion radiating from her face intensifies. "I don't understand, why would my mother be there?"

"She was the love of his life."

Her jaw sags, a puff of air escaping. "And did my mother … did she feel the same way?"

"I believe so." I hesitate, forcing myself to hold Aislinn's gaze that still swirls with questions and doubt. Questions I can handle. But doubt ... I cannot allow her to doubt me. "Ace Byrne is your father."

chapter twenty three

Aislinn

Before Marisol, I had another nanny, a woman who only lasted a week or so. Colleen was from Ireland, and she pronounced my name *Ash-lynn* rather than *Ace-lynn*. I thought my name sounded so pretty rolling off her tongue that way, but my mother corrected her every time. Eventually, Colleen apologized, saying that she was having a hard time because in Ireland, the correct pronunciation is actually *Ash-lynn*.

When I returned from school to find Colleen gone, her room empty, I asked my mother where she went. Her only response was, "I named you Aislinn for a reason, and if that girl can't pronounce it as I intended, we'll find someone who will."

My mother never did tell me what that reason was, and Marisol appeared the next day.

Ace Byrne is your—

I shake my head to clear the cobwebs before looking back up at Damon. "Does my father know?"

His face softens. "Yes."

It makes sense. So much sense. But any comfort I might have felt at the pieces finally coming together is far outweighed by grief that wraps around me like a wet wool blanket, cold and itchy. Not because my biological father is dead, although that is a weight poised to fall, sooner rather than later. But because the distance between me and the only father I've ever known, one I hoped to close by working together, by becoming a valuable member of his team, isn't one he'll ever let me cross.

My biology is something he's held against me. It's wrapped up in whatever happened between him and my mother. Whatever bond was broken between them, years ago, is now my fault. My problem. One that, in all likelihood, is permanent. Unfixable.

And *that* is what I'm mourning right now.

I am still reeling when I look back up at Damon. "How long? How long has he known?"

He smooths a wayward hair from my face with a gentle touch. "I don't know. That's something you'll have to ask him yourself when you're ready."

Will I ever be ready? Will my father tell me the truth when—*if*—I am? Is there even a chance my mother can shed light on their tangled history, my history?

Damon pushes out a heavy sigh and swings his legs over the edge of the mattress. "You need to sleep. I'll handle things from here."

I scramble after him, a sheen of tears blurring my vision. "No way. You are not shutting me out. Not now, not again."

I've put my trust in Damon and I refuse to be proven wrong. Too much has happened between us, because of us. I didn't come back just to be locked in Damon's apartment like a princess in an ivory tower. "We're either in this together, or we're nothing."

"I'm not shutting you out. I'm giving you time to recover,

to heal." He wraps a strand of my hair around his finger and tugs on it gently. "And we're not fucking *nothing*. There are simply things in my life you don't need to see. Ugliness I want to shield you from. I'm the corrupt King, remember? Now you know who I am and what I do. You don't need to see it, too."

I step in close to Damon's body, releasing my hold on the duvet I'd been clutching so tightly to my chest. "I see you, Damon. I've always seen you. Now I just see a little deeper is all." Extending my arms, I cup my palms on either side of his face, my thumbs sweeping across the aristocratic crest of his cheekbones. "Even the darkness in you is beautiful to me, Damon. You are my dark prince, my vengeful devil, my corrupt savior. And when you look at me, you only need to know one thing."

I wait for his eyes to sweep over every naked inch of me. My nipples are peaked with arousal, my normally fair skin flushed from the poignant throbbing between my thighs, my lips parted to allow my tongue to slide between the crease.

"What?" His one word question is a gritty rasp.

"I am yours, Damon King. All yours."

His features tighten as he pins me with an intense stare. "Do you mean that?"

I don't expect the question, or the sharp tone of his voice. And I hate the trace of doubt that darkens his gaze, pulling at his lips and leaving shadows beneath his eyes. But I answer plainly, honestly. "I do."

Damon hesitates, a wash of emotions flitting over his face. Joy cut by pain. Skepticism diluted by trust. "You deserve to live in the light, princess, because you are the sun. You deserve spotlights and chandeliers and flashing cameras. That's the life you were meant for."

"Maybe." I hike up on my toes to brush my lips across Damon's, a shiver traveling through me. "But with you, I have fireworks. So much better."

The bob of his Adam's apple hits me somewhere deep. "And that's enough for you? Are you sure?"

Damon King.

Fireworks.

"Yes. It's more than enough. *You're* more than enough."

He's everything. My everything.

chapter twenty four

Damon

A disquieting mix of gratitude and reluctance flows through my veins as the elevator descends to my underground office. Emotions that only intensify when Aislinn slips her small hand into mine.

And squeezes.

Like she's giving me reassurance.

I look down to see a grin trembling on her lips. A *reassuring* grin.

Jesus Fucking Christ. After what Aislinn's been through—she should be cursing me. Hell, she should be running in the opposite direction. Far and fast.

After what I just told her, Aislinn should be taking some time to herself. To rest, to heal, to process everything that's been thrown at her in the past week and a half.

Instead, she's right by my side. And I don't doubt that if I had attempted to leave my bedroom alone, she would have jumped on my back and clung to me like a monkey.

I'm still trying to figure out what to say—some way to explain what she's about to walk into—when the elevator door opens and Aislinn does indeed walk into it.

For a moment, I see everything through her eyes. The cement floor and exposed pipes. The walls covered in flat screens. The rows and rows of computers. Towers of hard drives with their flashing green and red lights.

But as we move away from the elevator, the low hum of voices cuts to silence as everyone swivels around to stare at the new face in their midst. Instinctively, Aislinn takes a step toward me, her upper arm pressing against my side. I slide a hand to her lower back, my fingers curling around her waist.

And then it's my turn to give Aislinn a reassuring squeeze.

I don't know what I'm doing. Right now, I barely know who the fuck I am.

But this girl right here, Aislinn Granville, I do know that she's mine. All mine.

She even told me so herself.

My eyes land on Finley's just as I hear a gasp coming from Aislinn.

She's staring over Finley's head at the pictures taken of the estate. The enormous house, landscaped grounds, and imposing wrought iron gates.

The man sprawled on a stone patio, the stones above his shoulders stained a deep cherry red.

Another man with a bullet wound through his forehead, slumped against the balcony railing.

The crumpled Jeep with a third, obviously dead man in the passenger seat.

I wrap my arm around Aislinn, expecting her to turn away, to press her face into my chest. But instead, she points at one screen in particular. "Where's Michael?" Her voice is breathless and thready, her stare unblinking.

"Michael?"

"The guy who was driving the Jeep. Michael. He—he was the dog walker."

"How many were at the house with you?"

"Five. Three guards, Sebastián, and Michael."

I look to Finley. "Find him."

She nods, one finger already tapping her headset. "On it."

I gently guide Aislinn to my office and close the door. She crosses her arms over her chest and rubs her arms as if she's chilled. "What is this place?"

I can spend the next few hours explaining all about heat expenditures and energy requirements of my operation, and the reasons I've chosen the bowels of New York City as my headquarters. But I have more pressing concerns. I loop my arms around her waist, sharing my warmth. "I'd like to bring your mother here."

Aislinn seems momentarily taken aback, but she regains her composure quickly. "Is that really necessary? She doesn't do well in new places. She'll be confused and upset. We can't do that to her."

I expected that. "Okay. I'll speak to your father about getting a team inside their home."

She looks away from me and worries at her lower lip. "That's definitely better ... but what about Marisol? She doesn't do well around most men, especially those carrying weapons."

"There are women on my payroll. I'll have them stationed inside. They'll be armed, of course, but—"

"That's fine. Does he know I was taken?"

"Yes. Cruz made contact with Lytton and I've been keeping tabs on their communication." Using his phone, I attempted to engage Cruz, but his only response was a once-daily photograph of Aislinn holding that day's newspaper.

"You've spoken with my father?"

I nod. "Yes."

"Was he—was he worried about me?"

My heart aches for the insecurity threaded through

Aislinn's tone. "Yes. We all were." I exhale a frustrated breath of air. "The photos kept me from losing my mind. But not knowing exactly what condition you were being kept ... I—"

She covers my mouth with her fingers. "That's behind us now." Her hand drops and for a moment I simply take comfort in her proximity, breathing in the sweetness of her scent.

"I want to know more about Ace."

Her question breaks me out of my trance. "I told you—"

"I'm not asking about my mother's relationship with Ace. I want to know yours. About how you and I intersect."

I swallow heavily. Recalling the photographs of a beautiful blonde taped to the pockmarked walls of a prison cell. "Ace asked me to keep an eye on you when I got out. You were a student at Columbia. It wasn't hard for me to blend in on campus, audit a few courses."

"You *watched* me?"

"A little." Enough to realize that the pictures on the wall didn't do Aislinn Granville justice. She was smart and kind and compassionate. A ray of light and life in a dark, drab world. Volunteering at a women's shelter and for Davina's organization.

Aislinn purses her full lips. "So, that's it. You kept an eye on me for Ace."

"Kind of. I never planned to do anything more than that." I make a sweeping gesture with my arms. "What kind of life can I give you, Aislinn? Look at what I've brought you into."

Understanding creeps into her expression, grabbing hold of her features. "There was no political operative looking to destroy my father's career, was there? The audio recording ... that was you, right?"

Staring into Aislinn's true blue eyes, I want to deny it. But I can't. "I'm sorry, princess." I push my fingers into the hair at the back of her neck, my wrists resting on the subtle rise of her shoulders as I kiss the groove that appears between her brows. "I fucking hate being the guy that puts this frown on your face."

"Then tell me the truth. Why the elaborate deception? Why go to all that trouble when—"

"Would you have believed me?" I interrupt. "I know about criminals. It's what I do. And when your father and Chad started cracking down on Los Muertos, I couldn't take the chance of you getting hurt. I had to step in—and I did it the only way I knew how."

"By lying."

I offer a shallow nod, my heart thudding as I stare into Aislinn's deep blue eyes. "And I'd do it again. At that moment, a lie was what I believed would keep you safe. We all make choices, Aislinn. Every minute of every goddamn day."

I pause, slowing down the cadence of my speech for emphasis. "Know this, I will choose you. Any day, any time. Every time. It's always been you. Nothing and no one is more important to me than you are."

"What about Finley?"

I blink, my brows drawing together. "Finley?"

"Yes. What do you really know about her?"

Does Aislinn suspect ...? "What are you asking?"

"I think she's the mole."

"I think this mole bullshit is a lie." I had my doubts about Finley after Aislinn was taken and they'd been completely disproved. "Just Sebastián Cruz trying to get inside your head."

She crosses her arms and glares at me. "That's not what he's doing."

"Oh no?"

"No."

"So, you're taking his word over mine?"

She throws up her hands. "For God's sake, he saved my life."

I go still. The implication of her reply smacking me in the face. The truth tearing me apart inside.

And. I. Didn't.

Not this time.

Sebastián Fucking Cruz took her and saved her and returned her.

I hate him. I owe him. I will destroy him.

Aislinn distracts from my anguished thoughts by throwing her arms around me. "Hey," she whispers, her hands cupping my face as she forces my gaze to hers. "I came back to *you*. I'm here with *you*. I would never have married Sebastián, ever."

The thought of Aislinn promising herself to another man is a lightning rod prodding my balls. The jolt so fierce and intense, for a moment my vision goes dark, my equilibrium swept aside.

Our foreheads have gravitated toward each other, our lips hovering just inches apart. We are breathing each other in, sharing each other's air, our breaths becoming one. This moment feels more intimate than a kiss. More intimate than what we did upstairs. Aislinn is like an extra atom of oxygen in the atmosphere. My lungs are full, my veins buzzing with a peculiar mix of gratitude and excitement.

Slowly, I lower myself to one knee. Grounded by one incontrovertible truth. "You will not marry anyone else but me, princess."

chapter twenty five

Aislinn

The blood drains from my face as I look down at Damon. "What are you doing? Get up."

He shakes his head. "I mean it. Marry me."

My mouth goes dry, the muscles lining my throat compressing my airway. "Why?" It's all I manage to say, despite the dozen other words blazing through my mind like a meteor shower.

"If Cruz is using you as Sebastián's *entré* into New York society, he'll want vows exchanged in front of everyone who is anyone in this city. And he's devout enough to insist on a church wedding."

Ignoring the absurdity of a pious drug lord, I follow Damon's train of thought. "And no priest will marry a woman who is already married in the eyes of God."

"Exactly. You would have to get an annulment, and those take time." He reaches for my hand and plants a kiss on the inside of my wrist. "Let's do this. It's an easy obstacle to throw in Cruz's path."

I pull my hand from Damon's grasp, turning away before

he can see me wince. *This* is his proposal? I feel … cheated.

I take a few steps away from him, needing a moment to sort through my thoughts.

If Chad had actually proposed, and I said yes, I would have been cheating myself.

If I had taken Sebastián's proposal seriously, our marriage would have been a lie.

However, making a commitment to Damon, and receiving one in return, isn't an unpleasant concept.

Not at all.

Unlike with Sebastián and Chad, I don't recoil in horror at the thought of marrying Damon. In fact, there is a strange surge of possessiveness that wraps around my brainstem. *This man is mine.*

Damon King is no storybook prince, and yet he makes me crave a picture perfect, happily ever after ending.

He is the man of my dreams.

The devil who danced into my heart, the monster who slayed my nightmares, the lover of my fantasies.

I turn back around to find Damon still on one knee, staring at me expectantly. Like a punch to the stomach, it hits me.

I love Damon King.

A love that is clearly unrequited. His proposal is merely a solution, an obstacle to throw in Cruz's path.

I clear my throat in an attempt to dislodge the hurt clogging it. "Is that all marriage is to you, a weapon in your arsenal?"

He rises to his feet slowly, until he towers over me once again. "What are you really asking?"

I don't want to ask Damon about his feelings for me. Because if he doesn't feel the same way, I'm not sure I could handle the answer.

And because I want him to tell me, on his own. But the

question sits on my tongue, and it won't be swallowed down. "I need—I need to know ..."

"What? Tell me."

I sigh, looking him straight in the eye and trying to fight the gravitational pull that makes me want to throw myself into his arms. "The truth, Damon. It's all I've ever needed."

He hesitates for a moment before admitting, "I care for you, Aislinn."

My blood heats, racing through my veins. I briefly wonder if the blue veins that crisscross the skin on the inside of my wrists have turned pink. "You *care* for me? Like I'm a patient you're responsible for—or a penniless orphan you feel obligated to support?"

He looks at me in bewilderment. "Of course not."

"Then what? You'll divorce me next month or next year or whenever Hugo Cruz decides I'm not worth the trouble?"

His expression becomes a scowl, and he takes a step back. "We're not married yet and you're already talking about a divorce?"

I run a trembling hand through my hair, turning away and averting my face from Damon's penetrating gaze. "Why not? I mean, if vows to honor and cherish each other won't actually mean anything—"

Damon grabs me by the elbow, spinning me around to face him. "Aislinn, I've honored and cherished you since before you knew my name. When I speak those vows, I will mean them. Because I already do."

The breath catches in the back of my throat. "You do?"

"Yes." He looks away. "But I don't expect you to feel the same way ..."

Damon's words are straightforward even as they trail off into silence, the expression on his face earnest. And suddenly, all I want to do is fall at his feet and grieve. This incredible man has been made to feel like a burden for most of his life.

I take his face into my hands, running my thumb over his weathered and stubbled skin, his strong jaw jutting into my palm. And I whisper, "You are worthy, Damon."

A long moment passes as we simply stare into each other's eyes. My blue meeting his brown. There is no heated clash, no battle of wills.

Just a softening as frothy bubbles of hope tickle my skin, like foam from the surf.

I love this man. Maybe Damon doesn't love me yet, or maybe he just doesn't realize he loves me yet. Either way, my love is big and strong and bold enough for the both of us. "Okay then. My answer is y—"

The door flies open, Burke stopping short at the threshold. "Sorry, boss. Didn't mean to interrupt."

Damon glances over at him. "Actually, I think you're just in time to hear Aislinn agree to be my wife." His head swivels back to me. "Yes?"

"Yes," I repeat, a laugh breaking free from the tightness in my chest. "Yes."

Damon pulls me into his arms. Our lips meet just as the quiet click of the door signals that we're alone again.

And then he drops to his knees at my feet, his head pushing between my thighs. My shirt is pushed up, my thong no defense against Damon's strong fingers. The flimsy lace rips in two just a moment before his thick tongue laves my already damp folds.

I steady myself on the desk behind me, my head dropping back as an exultant sigh shudders from my chest. Damon's wide palms support my ass, his thumbs holding me apart so that I am completely exposed.

That's what I am. With Damon, I am exposed. Vulnerable.

My inhibitions swept entirely aside.

And yet, entirely content in his arms.

Each pass of his tongue, each suck of my clit, each hungry grunt as Damon devours the most intimate part of me unravels another layer of my control.

Until there is none left and I can only gasp and tremble, lost to this moment.

Lost to this man.

chapter twenty-six

Aislinn

I regret making the call as soon as I hear my father's voice. "Hey, Dad," I begin.

"Aislinn?" He says my name like a question. "Where are you?"

"I'm h—I'm with King right now, at his place."

He grunts. "You're causing an awful lot of trouble for me lately."

I make a conscious decision to ignore his comment. "I have news. Damon and I are getting married."

"What?"

"Damon and I—"

"Jesus Christ, I heard what you said. The answer is no, goddamn it. I have plans for you and they don't include King."

I didn't call to ask my father's permission, but that doesn't make his refusal to give it any less hurtful. "We're getting married." My tone is quiet but firm. "Today, actually."

"Did you not hear me? I said no. Forget it."

"I heard you, but this is my choice. Damon is my choice."

There is a pause, a long one. And then, "You ungrateful bitch. I could have left you and your mother on the street twenty years ago. But I didn't, and this is how you repay me?"

My eyes flick to Damon's. His face is impassive, but my father is speaking so loudly I know he can hear every word. He holds out his hand for the phone, and I consider giving it to him. But ultimately, this exchange isn't about the man I've agreed to marry.

This is a conversation meant for two people. My father, a man so blinded by greed and betrayal he is incapable of unconditional love. And me, a daughter who must finally face the truth.

"I'm sorry you feel that way. Please give my love to—"

"Your mother?" His wry chuckle grates on my ears. "I should have known you would fall for a criminal. Like mother like daughter."

The call is dropped and I blow out a weary sigh, handing Damon his phone. "He's not coming."

I know not to bother calling Marisol. I am certain my father is already on the line with her, warning her against bringing my mother here, even if she was having a rare good day.

Damon gently sweeps a finger beneath my chin. I lift my head to meet his concerned gaze, blinking back tears. "It's fine. I'm fine, really."

But the tears don't dry up. They keep coming, overflowing my lashes and spilling down my cheeks. Damon's hands move to my cheeks, his thumbs swiping at the wetness until my tears run down his palms, dampening the cuffs of his sleeves. "I don't even know why I'm crying. I mean, nothing has really changed. Right?"

It's true. I know it's true. But James Granville is the man who raised me. Whether or not we share the same DNA doesn't matter to me. I'd wanted my father at my wedding.

So much has happened these past two weeks. My life has been turned upside down. I've faced uncomfortable truths about my parents, about my parentage. I've been assaulted and kidnapped. I've seen men killed. I've killed a man. The man I once believed to be my enemy became my lover. And soon, my husband.

I've faced all of that with barely a blink of an eye.

But this one thing—my father's disgusted dismissal—is too much. The final lash of a storm that sends me sprawling.

"Sometimes there's little difference between nothing and everything, princess." Damon gives up on trying to dry my tears and instead pulls me into his chest, wrapping his arms around my back, his fingers running through my hair in a gentle, soothing rhythm.

A soggy laugh gurgles from my throat as I push my face into the crisp cotton of Damon's shirt. The statement makes no sense and perfect sense at the same time.

A rush of gratitude washes over me. Damon has the ability to make me feel like everything will be okay, even though my life has completely fallen apart. Not long ago, I hated him. Now, I can't imagine my life without him.

I've craved attention my whole life. Craved it like a flower stretching toward the sun. But I've lived in the shadow of my famous father and his political ambitions for so long, I don't even know what to do with the unrelenting rays Damon shines my way.

It feels too strong. Too intense. But also, so damn good. I am warmed all the way to my bones.

Making it easier to ignore the ice pick still niggling at my brain. *Does my husband-to-be love me?*

I turn in Damon's arms so I can face him. "So, where do we go from here?"

chapter twenty-seven

Damon

"I do."

Those two tiny words take on considerably more significance when said in front of a judge.

"Then, by the power invested in me by the state of New York, I now pronounce you husband and wife." A hot surge of protectiveness rises up in my chest as I look into Aislinn's face. "You may now kiss the bride."

We're not in a church. And she's not wearing a wedding gown.

But I am certain no one has ever spoken more sacred vows.

Aislinn and I have kissed many times, but this time feels different. It is different. Aislinn Granville is now Aislinn King. My wife.

My queen.

I drag her body against mine, swallowing her low moan with a louder groan. Soft and willowy, Aislinn yields to me, her spine as supple as her spirit is fierce.

Burke and Finley, our two witnesses, applaud as the judge

looks on impatiently. My summons was an unwanted surprise. He is clearly eager to leave and wash his hands of the whole business. Which he does, the second we break apart.

Not that it matters. He's served his purpose. Aislinn is now mine. No man will ever touch her or kiss her or hurt her—ever again. All this bullshit about Aislinn marrying Sebastián Cruz to forge a bond between their families is now a moot point.

This girl belongs to me. Forever.

After the judge rushes out, Burke pops a bottle of champagne. A Krug Clos D'Ambonnay I bought at auction several years ago. I'd been saving it for a special occasion, and this definitely qualifies.

Finley passes out the brimming flutes. I open my mouth to make a toast but Burke beats me to it. "To an enchanting bride and her rather undeserving king. May you both live happily ever after."

My scowl is slightly softened by the flash of the enormous diamond on Aislinn's finger as she lifts her glass, the open smile on her face more brilliant than any gemstone.

Once Aislinn agreed to marry me, Burke was sent to retrieve the judge while Finley brought a jeweler. Not just any jeweler, of course. Harry Winston. The best.

My instructions were specific. A ring suitable for a spitfire. Jewels that radiate fire and sun and light and beauty.

He came with a suitcase of rings, and I found the one I wanted instantly. A deep, canary yellow emerald-cut diamond, surrounded by burnt amber trillions. It is bold and beautiful. Unique.

Just like Aislinn.

"All right, you crazy kids, where's the honeymoon?"

I glare at Burke. "I think we have our hands full here in New York for the moment."

"All work and no play." He looks at Aislinn. "Please tell me you'll take him away sometime soon. Finley and I can hold down the fort while you two sip umbrella drinks in the sun."

I watch as Aislinn takes a sip of her champagne, a solitary bubble lingering tantalizingly on her upper lip until she swipes it with her tongue. A pang of desire hits south of my belt buckle.

"I don't know if my new husband is an umbrella drink kind of guy." She turns to me with an adorably arched brow. "Is he?"

"No. I can assure you, he is not," I respond in the third person.

She makes a *we'll see* sound and winks at Burke. "He'll be the first one in line for a piña colada, I just know it."

Finley adds, "Umbrella or not, I don't see you going anywhere you'll have to wait in line."

I lift my glass. Finley knows me well. "True." I toss back what remains of my champagne and set down the glass.

And then I sweep my bride into my arms, carrying her back to my bed.

Our bed.

chapter twenty eight

Aislinn

I am on fire from the inside out. Our vows were tinder, primed to explode into flames from the first brush of Damon's lips against mine. From the sparks lighting up at every point of contact.

This ache inside me can only be soothed by one man.

My man.

My monster.

My king.

My husband.

"Wife," Damon growls, just as he drops me into the center of the bed. "It's time to consummate our marriage."

God, even the word *consummate* sounds sexy coming from Damon's lips. And the way he looks at me, his dark, burning eyes sweeping over every inch of my body, his lips curling up in a possessive smile as if I'm a gift. A gift he's longed for.

His gift.

I rise up on my knees, unbuttoning buttons, unclasping clasps, pushing down straps. Until there's not a single piece of fabric covering my body. Until the desperate buds of my nipples peek through the mounds of hair falling over my shoulders in rippling blonde waves.

Damon makes quick work of his clothes, each movement smoothly efficient. The muscles beneath his skin flex and bunch in a graceful display of power, a living work of art. He sets one knee down on the mattress, then the other, the tips of his fingers lightly stroking the flare of my waist, the length of my thighs, the teardrop curves of my breasts.

And then they slide up to my face, his palms cradling my cheeks. "I am going to worship you, every day of my life."

"For better or worse?" There's a hint of a tease in my voice, because I don't know how to respond to the raw passion bleeding from his.

"No. There will only be better. Every day we share will be better than the one that's come before."

And maybe because we've already faced so many bad days together, I believe him.

His hands shift slightly, his fingers pushing past my temples so that he's supporting my weight as I arch back, my breasts grazing his chest with each gulped inhale.

Electricity crackles between us, a potent energy that sizzles over my skin.

My mouth is already open when his face descends to mine, a meeting of lips and teeth and tongues that feels like the secret door to another dimension. Because I am falling through a void, lost to everything but Damon's kiss, Damon's touch. Damon himself.

I moan as we melt into the bed, an intricate tangle of limbs loosely knotted together and yet permanent all the same. Because this, *us*, feels like forever.

I'm sure of it.

There are still threats. A thousand miles away, Hugo Cruz is plotting revenge. And just downstairs, someone in Damon's organization is conspiring to take down my king.

Let them try.

Tonight, we will revel in our union, celebrate our victory. Tomorrow, we will do what needs to be done. Together.

"Fuck, princess." My hips roll as I wrap my legs around Damon's narrow hips, interlocking my ankles as I press the thick bulge of his cock between my thighs. I am impatient and greedy and I want nothing more than to be joined physically, to be filled and stretched in the most delicious way.

"Fuck me, husband," I demand. This time it's my hands that curve around his face, my thumbs that sweep across the jutting blades of his cheekbones, my gaze that blazes with adoration. There is so much emotion inside my chest it's cracking open from the volume of it. "Fuck me like my monster. Like my king."

Fuck me like you love me.

Because on this night, our wedding night, I need to believe he does.

Damon enters me slowly, a luxuriously thick slide that has me curling my fingernails into the back of his neck as I arch up against him. He dips his head, pulling one nipple into his mouth, then the other.

Pleasure winds within me like a corkscrew. A sharp, pointed, almost painful press through my chest.

There is no beginning to this sensation, and I can't fathom an end. Just an inexorable turning. Twisting. Breaking apart and fusing together.

Until I split entirely in two. A wide open crack that has me gasping and crying. The seam just long and wide enough for Damon to slip beneath my skin, lodging somewhere deep inside my chest, right beside my heart.

It is only hours later, with Damon's arms wrapped around me and his sleepy breaths fanning my hair against my neck, knowing he won't hear them, that I dare to breathe the words

I've wanted to say all day. Maybe even longer.

I love you.

chapter twenty-nine

Damon

I haven't been in my office long when I'm told Aislinn is demanding to be allowed downstairs. I chuckle, hearing her irate tone in the background. "Mrs. King has free rein. She may go wherever she wishes."

I'm leaning against one of the pillars opposite the elevator doors when she bursts through them. "You should have woken me."

"Because that ring on your finger turned you into a morning person?"

"Because you need me." She steps in close, lowering her voice to a whisper. "Someone on your team is trying to take you down. You need my help."

"I've already gone through everyone on my payroll. Sebastián lied to you."

Her eyes flare. "That's exactly why you need me. Your judgment is tainted."

I grab Aislinn's hand and pull her into my office, closing the door and tapping a few commands on my computer. An image of Burke appears on my screen. "Former Navy Seal.

Been with me for years. Saved my life as many times as I've saved his."

I press another key. "Justin and Tim. The guys you just railed at upstairs. Both former special forces. Justin's kid has a rare blood disease, but he hasn't seen a medical bill since the day he started working for me. Tim was recruited by Burke, they grew up on the same block and have known each other for thirty years."

I pull up another image. "Juliana is the daughter of the first woman The Network relocated. Because of me, she grew up without having to watch her father beat the shit out of her mother every night."

Aislinn inserts herself between me and the keyboard. "That's not the way this works. I can't clear someone based on a two-sentence bio from you. I need a complete list of your staff and a workstation that's not linked to your network."

"Fine. I'll tell Finley."

"No. You can't tell anyone what I'm doing, especially Finley."

"Especially Finley?" I repeat with a raised brow.

Aislinn stands her ground. "Yes."

"I thought you two were getting along."

"We are," she says with a toss of her hair. "It's nothing personal, Damon. This is business."

I bristle. "*My* business."

"Yes. And you should be thanking me for offering my services."

"Why are you doing this, Aislinn? You've made it perfectly clear you disagree with my methods. That you hate corruption and crime and dirty politics. What's changed?"

"I married you. I chose you. And just because I don't agree with you, doesn't mean I'm going to let someone hurt you."

I have to bite my lip to hold back a pleased grin.

My spitfire is standing up to me ... to protect me.

Not because I'm her boss. Not because she's on my payroll.

But because I'm *hers*.

chapter thirty

Aislinn

"You can change your mind, Aislinn. From what I understand, it's a woman's prerogative." Damon's knowing stare reads my discomfort as we stand outside a seedy, Lower East Side strip club.

But the sexy smirk twisting his lips has me squaring my shoulders and straightening my spine. Getting back into Damon's car, cowering behind tinted windows until I can hide inside his luxury apartment, isn't an option.

I spent most of the day working in Damon's office. He was in and out throughout much of it, but when he tried to leave after a late dinner together, I insisted on joining him. I'm not backing out now.

My eyes flash. "Not this woman." I step around his overprotective bulk. The bouncer guarding the door makes no move to open it until Damon's standing beside me, then he does so with a deferential nod as if our entry was never in doubt.

My sole experience with strip clubs is what I've seen on TV and in the movies. Some characteristics are as I expect.

A brightly lit narrow platform bisects the room, a silver pole at the end of it. The perimeter is in shadow, the male audience only vaguely discernible. A beautiful woman with long hair and lush curves gyrates enthusiastically to loud music.

Deep booths line one wall, a bar lines another, and high-top tables fill in the rest of the space.

But cameras can't capture the smell of cheap perfume, heavy aftershave, and strong liquor that hits me like a foul, humid wall.

This place is unsettling—the loud music and harsh lights and deep shadows. The heady scents and underdressed women. The men staring intently at the stage, some with one hand beneath the table in front of them.

Damon's palm is a comforting presence at my lower back, and I look up at him. The smirk that bothered me just moments earlier has softened slightly. More determined confidence than pure cockiness. Damon edges ahead of me, his hand sliding along my waist as he leads me toward a large corner booth.

My nerves jangle beneath my skin when he comes to a stop in front of it, the low rumble that emerges from his chest not a language I recognize. Russian, maybe. A minute passes as words are exchanged, and then Damon slides into one side of the booth, pulling me with him.

He doesn't make any introductions, although five pairs of eyes flick to me, but only briefly. Damon reaches an arm across my thighs and practically growls before saying something that sounds a hell of a lot like *she's mine*.

There is a bottle of vodka in the middle of the table and one of the men takes two fresh glasses, filling them to the brim. There are no mixers, no lime wedges. But I gulp at it anyway, trying not to cough as it sears a path down my esophagus. Damon pours it down his throat in one toss, not

SAVIOR

flinching at all.

As the conversation continues, my attention drifts to the women who strut and crawl and dance in the center of the room. Their faces are impassive, their choreography not particularly artful. I can't help but wonder what they are thinking as they dance to an audience of rapt, gaping men. The ones seated near the stage clutch cocktail glasses in one hand and wads of cash in their others, only setting down their drinks to stuff bills into tiny G-strings.

After a few songs, I realize that the dancers circulate among the crowd when they're not on stage. Their faces now wearing bright smiles, as painted-on as their harsh makeup.

The vodka is strong, but the burn as it splashes down my throat decreases with each sip.

The guttural conversation flowing around me fades into the background as I imagine myself on stage. Dancing and stripping and flaunting myself—but only for an audience of one. Damon King.

My thighs edge apart as I lean forward, placing my elbows on the table, my hands balling into fists as I use them to prop up my chin. I am entirely too aware of Damon's possessive hand covering my left knee, the sweep of his thumb on the bare skin of my inner thigh. I squirm beneath his touch, wishing he would move his fingers closer to my core, wanting him to feel my heat, drag his fingertips through my increasingly damp folds.

I am not drunk, merely buzzed. A buzz that softens the edges of the room, the blare of the music, the harshness of this day. Even so, there is a tawdry sadness to this place that hovers like dense smog.

One of the men Damon's been talking to slams his hand on the table, startling me. I jump, sending Damon's grip to mid-thigh. I don't bother attempting to stifle my moan. It's covered by the heavy bass that vibrates through the seat of the booth.

The action wasn't done in anger though, as the men, Damon included, all lift their glasses and throw their heads back. I do the same, although I was clearly not a part of the toast.

At Damon's nudge I slide out of the booth and am surprised when he leads me to the back instead of toward the front, the way we came in. "Where are we going?"

Damon doesn't answer. He stops at an open door. One of his men is in there. "Are we clear?" Damon asks.

The man checks a device in his hands and gives a firm nod. "Yes." He walks past us, closing the door behind him. I know without asking that he will remain right outside.

I look at Damon again. "What are we doing?"

"Giving the Albanians half an hour to put together a plan and agree to my offer." His lips twitch. "Your skin was on fucking fire out there, Aislinn. Thought I'd give you the chance to try out some of those moves you were studying so intently. On me."

My jaw sags when I finally take in the space he's brought me to. It's about the same size as my closet in Damon's apartment. There is a small stage in the center of the room, and a vertical pole that extends to the ceiling. Opposite, a dark couch blends in with the dark walls. "You brought me back here to ... strip for you?"

He grunts. "I brought you back here so you wouldn't bum rush the stage." His hands grip my shoulders, exerting just enough force so that I step slowly backward until my spine is pressed against the pole. "Tell me I won't find you wet and wanting beneath your skirt, Aislinn."

I clench my thighs together but know it would be futile. A flush rises up my cheeks and I dip my head. "How can we be sure—"

I break off when Damon's fingers gather my chin and lift

my gaze to his. "I had the room swept for recording equipment. We're alone."

After a kiss that is firm and quick but still manages to leave me whirling, Damon sinks into the couch, his feet firmly planted on the floor, powerful thighs spread slightly apart. As I gather my composure, he watches me from beneath hooded eyes. I can see the length of him, thick and distinct, outlined against the fabric of his suit pants.

Music is also pumped into this room, although it feels less abrasive on my ears here. "I'm not a dancer," I say. "I don't know what to do."

Neither of those statements is exactly true. I do have years of dance training. Ballet, jazz, ballroom. The dance floor was one of the few places I felt free as a kid. Unrestrained. But it's been years since I've trained. I spent time on a stripper pole more recently. Not at an actual strip club, but at a trendy exercise studio I attended religiously for a while. But then my favorite instructor quit, and I lost interest.

Damon shrugs. "You are the most graceful woman I've ever seen. Give it a shot."

Give it a shot? Like twirling on a pole is something that comes naturally. It's not. Dancers make it look easy, but it takes hours and hours of training to look effortlessly sexy.

The classes I took were designed for exercise, and I was too busy trying not to fall off the pole to worry about being seductive.

A new song comes on, Beyoncé's latest, and I run my tongue between suddenly dry lips.

Give it a shot.

I take a deep breath, swallowing down my insecurities as I stare at the man in front of me. What's the worst that could happen? I trip and hurl myself into Damon's lap. Not such a bad outcome.

A fresh surge of lust floods my veins as my hips begin to

move, swaying from side to side. The muscles lining my diaphragm tense, engaging my core. My feet edge outward, my knees relaxing.

I reach behind my back for the pole, my hands closing around the cool metal. It feels good against my overheated palms. The music is too loud to hear my moan, but it vibrates inside my throat as I rub my ass against the pole through my skirt.

From across the room, Damon's eyes glitter at me like onyx stones. His expression is stoic, yet intensely focused. On me.

With one last glance at the closed door, I unbutton my skirt and pull at the zipper. It falls smoothly to the floor, forming a black ring around my feet. I run my hands along my naked thighs, undulating to the heavy bass. My shirt is next, and when it joins my skirt, I kick both to the side and walk around the pole, holding it with just one hand.

One rotation, then two. On the third, I kick up a leg and find purchase by hooking it around the pole, launching myself upward. Muscle memory takes over, the basic skills I learned in class now imbued with the sensual energy pulsing through my lungs with every beat of the music.

I know Damon is watching me, and I know this dance is for him.

But there's no room for anyone else on the pole but me. I am not experienced enough to take my attention off what I am doing. I fly through the air, a whirling dervish with long, loose hair and high stiletto heels that punctuate every movement, every twist and turn and spin.

By the second chorus, the pole has become my lover. I grip it with my hands and thighs, dragging my belly and thong-covered pussy along its hard, silvery length.

I am the sum of my breaths and movements, the room a blur of bright spotlights, dark shadows, and the flash of the chrome pole. At some point, I manage to unclasp my bra, flinging it in Damon's general direction. With each sway of my breasts, an electric spark bursts to life between my thighs.

When the final beat of the song is pumped through the speakers, I swing my feet to the floor, blinking away the haze that descended on me during my performance. My thighs tremble from exertion as I slowly cross the room, the mist between me and Damon evaporating with each step.

His hungry stare rakes down my body, possessively marking every inch of me as his.

I am branded by it.

I throw my knees over the thickness of Damon's thighs, staring into his eyes as my fingers furiously work his belt buckle. I am drowning in a sea of lust. I need Damon's cock inside me, my soft filled by his hard, our bodies joined together. I want to ride him as fiercely as I did the pole. I want to explode with pleasure, erupt with passion.

I am his and he is mine. Husband and wife.

chapter thirty-one

Damon

Aislinn Granville—no, Aislinn King—is many things. Beautiful, smart, passionate, honest, loyal. I can stack adjective on top of adjective all the way to the fucking sky. But, when she dances, she is completely captivating. I can't pull my eyes away from her if I wanted to.

Not that I want to.

Her expression is one of fierce concentration, but there is joy too. Like the music and movement has freed something inside of her. Every action is graceful. And there is power within her dance. Strength.

It is a perfect encapsulation of Aislinn herself.

Why the fuck haven't I asked her to dance for me before?

After tonight, I should have a goddamn pole installed in our bedroom.

Her skin is flush with exertion when she straddles me. Her mouth slightly parted, breaths coming heavy, her hair a lush blonde tangle that falls over her shoulders and down her back, errant strands clinging to her dewy skin.

The attraction and energy between us sizzles in the air.

My dick is harder than it's ever been, painfully swollen inside my pants, leaking against my thigh. And in this seedy room, in this shitty strip club ... it feels as if we are the only two people in the world. Two tortured royals—an embattled, enraptured king and his captured queen. Everything that's happened has brought us here, to this place, this moment. Into each other's arms.

I suck in air through my teeth as she frees me, shoving my pants down my hips and fisting me just long enough to position my already cum-slick crown at her entrance.

"Christ," I swear, my body rigid as the tight, wet, heat of her glides over my length until her bare ass makes contact with the fabric of my trousers. A satisfied grin pulls at Aislinn's mouth as she throws her head back and groans, goose bumps spreading across her chest like a textured path directing me to her dusky pink nipples. I cup one breast in each hand, sucking and biting and teasing her nipples as she sets up a rhythm that starts slowly, sensually in tune with the music, and becomes frenzied and desperate. Her hips roll over me relentlessly, and I glance down at her sweetly winking belly button, knowing my cock must be just behind it.

We both come hard, needing relief. Desperate for it, actually. It didn't take long—hell, every second of her dance was foreplay. We were both so close to the brink that when she lowered herself onto my cock, it was almost painful, every second until she clenched around me, until I erupted inside her, excruciating.

Afterward, Aislinn slumps in my arms, her naked breasts heaving against my chest, her head pressed to my shoulder, her shuddering breaths fanning my neck. "Who needs a honeymoon?" she asks, the question mangled by a choked laugh.

"We do," I reply, running my fingers up and down the

notched ladder of Aislinn's spine, her hair weaving between each knuckle. "And I promise you, the Lower East Side isn't it."

She moans as I grip her shoulders and push her upright. "Since I intend to give you the honeymoon you deserve, let's get back out there. The sooner I strike a deal with the Albanians, the sooner we can get away."

chapter thirty two

Damon

I'm not surprised that the Albanians agree to my terms. They've wanted a stronger foothold in New York for years. I've resisted because of their involvement with the international sex trafficking trade.

Meanwhile, I've been charging the Albanians heavily for my protection. And although they haven't lost a dime of their drug or arms sales, I've never given advance warning of any raid or warrant related to trafficking. They will expect more from our relationship now. More diligence regarding a segment of their business I despise.

They won't get it.

I will use the Albanians to crush the Los Muertos cartel. Hugo Cruz will become a minor player in New York and the entire East Coast. I haven't decided what to do about Sebastián yet, but I do know that I will not rest until I've hunted down Michael myself. When the dust settles, and Michael's blood coats my hands, I will squash the Albanians like a fat tick.

"So, what now?" Aislinn asks once we are headed back to

my apartment.

"Nothing tonight. Unless Michael's location is pinpointed."

The shiver that trembles through Aislinn's bones at his name twists my stomach. "Do you expect that will happen soon?"

"I do. And princess, I'm not taking you with me. That man will never lay eyes on you again. I'll see to it personally."

"But—"

I lay a finger over her lips to prevent anything else from tumbling out. "It's not up for discussion."

Her eyes glint at me before she turns her head away, crossing her arms over her chest as her lips fuse into a tight line.

Aislinn is quiet as we undress and get into bed, offering no protest as I pull her against me. My cock instinctively stiffens again but I ignore it. What I really need is to hold Aislinn close as she falls asleep in my arms. I need to feel her pulse become languid, her breaths deep and even. I need to feel her ribcage rise and fall in a steady rhythm, her hair tickling my chest with each movement. I need her sweetness, her sunshine, her light eclipsing my dark.

Need.

I've never needed anything or anyone. And yet, I can't deny that I need Aislinn in my life. That she has become as necessary to my existence as oxygen.

The knowledge isn't a relief.

It's uncomfortable, a weight I don't trust myself to carry.

With a soft sigh, the last bit of tension leaves Aislinn's body as she drops off into sleep. Clearly, she doesn't share the same fear. Her trust is obvious.

Again, the knowledge isn't a relief.

chapter thirty three

Aislinn

I knew Damon wouldn't be beside me when I woke up, and I am right. He is gone.

A sense of foreboding scratches at my nerve endings, a knot of worry pulsing inside my stomach. Whatever deal Damon brokered yesterday is no doubt being carried out today ... but a feeling that things won't go as planned nags at me.

I can't pinpoint the reason, and I have no basis for it. But it's there.

With a muffled groan, I throw off the covers, and a piece of paper soars into the air from the nightstand, landing on my chest.

I've told Finley to expect you.

I read Damon's words once, twice. Trying to figure out if he's telling me to go downstairs, or merely implying I shouldn't let Finley scare me away.

He's left things open to interpretation. Maybe even deliberately vague.

I take my time in the shower and then dress slowly, blow-drying my hair until there's not a trace of dampness left behind. If not for that note I would have rushed downstairs, snapping at Finley's heels for any information she has, watching her every move. I still want a clear understanding of what she knows and what she does—but I'm through acting solely on impulse. It hasn't served me well.

No, I need to be deliberate. Strategic.

Yesterday I created dossiers on half the men in King's organization. Today I will work on the women. Starting with Finley.

If Hugo Cruz wants access to Damon's accounts, his best bet would be to recruit Finley as his mole.

I leave Damon's bedroom and step into the corridor. The men waiting outside escort me downstairs without a word of protest.

Finley's expression is inscrutable as I walk toward her. "Aislinn."

I nod politely. "Good morning." I look away from her and gesture at the screens lining the cement walls. "How are things going?"

"Things?"

"I would be more specific if I could." *But I can't, and Finley knows it.*

"Well, there's not much to report, I'm afraid. Damon hasn't checked in yet."

"Is that ..." My voice trails off as I swallow heavily, "unusual?"

Her shoulders lift in a barely there shrug. "Not really."

"Oh." It's a soft puff of air, and I look around for something else to talk about.

"Why don't you go hang out in Damon's office? I'll let you know if anything comes up."

Hang out? The dismissiveness of the phrase grates on my nerves. "Actually," I step around Finley to the empty workspace at her right, "I think I'll just *hang out* right here."

I notice a tic in her jaw, but she merely averts her eyes. "Suit yourself."

She spends the next hour ignoring me, but I don't bother pretending to do the same. It's interesting, watching Finley in her own environment. She's confident and decisive, and everyone speaks to her with respect.

It's also frustrating, because I don't know what I should be looking for. She could be sabotaging Damon right in front of me and I wouldn't have any idea.

But if I can't find something to expose Finley, maybe I can learn something from her.

I take notes on the laptop Damon gave to me, paying particular attention to the women on Damon's staff. There aren't many, and two of them are now at my parent's townhouse. That is, if my father hasn't thrown them out yet.

Gina and Nancy seem solely focused on Damon's global financial interests. Karen works on a team covering the NYPD database. And Juliana monitors Los Muertos communications between New York and Mexico, reporting directly to Finley.

My mind keeps returning to the secrets my parents have kept from me. "Do you know a man named Ace?" I ask the question during what feels like a lull, expecting another shrug and an irritated blow-off.

Instead, Finley's body goes entirely still, and she takes a full minute to turn her head in my direction. "Who?"

I blink at her. I know she heard me. More importantly, the name was clearly familiar to her. But I repeat it again. "Ace."

She rubs her chin and pretends to consider. "Maybe, I'm not sure. Why do you ask?"

I'm not about to blurt out that he's my father. "Apparently he's an old friend of my mother's. She mentioned his name the other day."

"Oh?" She looks intently at something on her computer screen. "What did she say about him?"

"Not much," I answer honestly.

She huffs an affronted breath, her fingers a sharp staccato on her keyboard as she mutters something inaudible.

"What?"

She lifts her hands suddenly, like a pianist after her solo. "I said, 'that's not surprising.'" Her words are clipped, her face flushed.

"How so?"

"Ace was in prison for years, just upstate. Your mother never visited him. Not even once, even though it was her fault he was there."

My head spins at Finley's angry tirade. "I don't—I don't understand. My mother sent Ace to prison?"

Her wry laugh has several heads spinning in our direction, but either Finley doesn't notice or doesn't care. "Technically, it was your father that sent Ace to prison. When he found out that he wasn't actually your father. Your mother did nothing to stop him. So, I guess it doesn't surprise me that she doesn't have much to say about him."

The fact that Finley knows the intimate details of my parentage—something I've only just learned myself—abrades my composure. I clear my throat, trying not to overreact. "The reason my mother can't talk to me about Ace is that she has Alzheimer's. She barely speaks at all anymore."

Finley blinks several times, the color in her cheeks fading. "I'm sorry. I didn't know."

"I guess that's not surprising, either," I reply, holding her stare. Assuming familiarity based on half-truths and innuendos is for slackers and fools. Finley is neither.

chapter thirty four

Damon

I learned how to pick a lock in prison and have improved my skills significantly over the years. Whether a simple cylinder mechanism or a more advanced electronic one, there are few I can't handle.

In less than two minutes I am inside the apartment. Normally I would have Burke with me, but not today. Today is for me.

I've learned quite a lot about Michael, whose full name is Michael Clark. The man is no dog walker, although his cousin ran a business training guard dogs. Until recently, Clark was Cruz's East Coast money launderer.

He must have been expecting me, because he gets a shot off when I am barely past the front door.

I feel the impact, of course. But I am too angry for pain. My Kevlar absorbs the blow, and instead of dropping to the ground, I leap on him. His second, and last, shot grazes my shoulder before I break his wrist and toss the gun aside.

His howl of pain is one of the most beautiful sounds I've ever heard. Music to my ears.

If I only wanted to kill Michael, he would be dead already. But my thirst for blood, for vengeance, is too strong to be satisfied with a quick kill.

No. Michael needs to suffer.

I knock him out sufficiently to put him into a thick black duffel bag. Breaking a bone or two in the process. Then I carry him out to my car, throw him in the back, and head to another building I own. I have a few underground workrooms spread throughout the city.

There isn't much in the way of comfort. Blood-stained cement floor. Blood-stained cement walls.

I drop the bag on the ground, satisfied by the heavy thud, a distinct *crack*.

When I pull back the zipper, Michael groans. I give him a swift kick with the tip of my boot. "Cruz will kill you," Michael wheezes.

I kneel down to look him in the face. "He should have killed me—before he took Aislinn. But … here I am."

I slam a closed hand into his cheekbone. "When Aislinn came back to me, she had a cut on her cheek."

Another hard jab to his eye.

"She had to look at your ugly face for four days."

A final punch to the center of his face.

"One of your men tried to rape her. Did you know that?"

Michael's skin is striped with his own blood. It leaks through the hands he uses to cover his face. I pull them aside, peering at him curiously.

"You will pay for every ounce of discomfort you caused my girl."

He shakes his head violently. "Blame Cruz, not me. Or Granville's lackey."

I still. "Who? I need a name."

"Lytton. He called me in for questioning, tried to get me to flip on Cruz. I refused, but the bastard put the word out that I agreed. Cruz didn't trust me, and he stopped running money through me. My days were numbered.

"I knew he'd tried to get the Granville girl twice already and failed. So I cut a deal with Cruz—my life in exchange for the girl."

Interesting. There is hope in Michael's eyes as he focuses on my smile. "Thanks for the intel," I say in a low voice, almost teasing. "But you're here now." He doesn't see my fist until it's too late. Landing on his lips, I feel the scrape of his teeth tearing at my skin as I knock them loose from his gums. Michael's scream ricochets off the cement, vibrating inside my ears.

The next few hours pass in a hazy blur, although my actions are mechanical and exacting.

This is a sentence I'm carrying out. Justice.

Vengeance.

And when he is finally just a lump on the ground, his breaths steady but labored, I take my knife and slice down his chest, my hand closing around his still beating heart. "This is for Aislinn." I pull the organ from his chest cavity and shove it inside his gaping mouth.

Later, after I've showered in the bathroom I had installed for similar occasions, I take a picture of Michael's almost unrecognizable face, encrypt the file and send it to Cruz via the dark net.

And then I set his body on fire.

Let the city rats feast on Michael Clark's roasted carcass tonight. He will be nothing but scorched remains and gnawed bones tomorrow.

chapter thirty-five

Aislinn

I spend the morning at Finley's side, peppering her with questions about ... everything. Damon's operation is complicated. Finance. Politics. Crime. There are so many moving parts and I'm determined to understand how each piece fits into the overall puzzle.

I don't agree with what he does, and I don't expect that I ever will. But reforming a corrupt organization requires intimate knowledge of that organization's operations. My interests are now aligned with Damon's, and while I don't expect to change *him*, I can't say the same for his business model.

I have other questions, too. Questions that have nothing to do with Damon. "When did Ace go to prison?"

"What does it matter?" she responds irritably, immersed in a complicated model forecasting foreign currency exchange rates.

"It matters," I snap back. "When?"

"Almost twenty years ago."

Right after my attack. A wave of nausea rocks into me and

I close my eyes.

"Are you going to get sick? Shit." A bottle of water is pressed into my hands. "Here, drink this."

I lift it to my lips and the cold liquid splashes over my tongue, washing away some of the bitterness that had risen up my throat. "Thank you," I mumble, clutching it in my hands like a lifeline.

"Sure." I can feel her worried eyes on me, although I'm not sure it's genuine concern. Finley probably just doesn't want to be blamed by Damon. "What's important about the timing?"

I hesitate before answering, unsure about opening up to a woman I barely know. A woman who may be working against Damon. Eventually, I sigh and decide to take a chance. "I was a real daddy's girl when I was young. But around twenty years ago, that changed. There was an incident, and I was taken to the hospital. I was fine, but I remember that they ran a lot of tests. Maybe that's when my father learned I wasn't his biological daughter."

"You think they did a DNA swab or something?"

"I—I'm not sure. But they definitely would have checked my blood type." I sighed. "I do know that things changed after that. My father and I had been close but when I got back home, he could barely look at me. I thought it was all my fault. That I did something to make him stop loving me."

"If that's true, would he have retaliated by putting Ace in prison?"

"Yes," I answer Finley's question quickly, then take another sip of water before rising unsteadily to my feet. "I think I should go back upstairs."

"You think you can make it there without falling down or puking?" She regards me skeptically, a faint trace of concern woven through her words.

I pull my shoulders back and take a deep breath. "I'll be

fine, Finley."

She stands too. "You got into politics in the hopes that your father would notice you, right? To become useful enough to have value?"

I wish I could deny it. Proclaim that my chosen career is some kind of calling. But I can't. I nod slowly. "Yeah. Pathetic, huh?"

The scorn I glimpsed in her face earlier isn't there anymore. I see only compassion and understanding. She shuffles closer to me, reaching out to pat my arm. It's awkward, almost as if physically touching someone is uncomfortable to her. "Kind of," she says with a flickering grin. "But I'm in the same boat. We're more alike than I would have guessed."

Any other day, I would have sat back down, kicked off my shoes, and gotten comfortable. But I am completely incapable of girl talk right now. Or any talk, really. "Looks like we have some common ground other than Damon."

She mumbles something affirmative and heads back to her desk.

I take a deep breath and continue toward the elevators, hoping that I haven't just blown my chance to get to know Finley a little better. Maybe if I get my shit together, we will actually become friends.

I think I'd like that. But can I trust her?

Each new fact I've learned about my parents, about myself, has left me feeling exposed and brittle. Like one of those manuscripts Sebastián studies. A strong wind could turn me into dust, scatter me into so many pieces I'll never be whole again.

Upstairs, hours pass. I reach for my phone a dozen times, never quite able to tap CALL. Even if Damon answers, I'm not going to be satisfied until he's standing in front of me.

I wander aimlessly around his apartment, stare anxiously

out windows, sit uneasily on chairs. I jump at the slightest noise. The high ceilings feel like they are pressing on my head, the enormous rooms claustrophobic.

Where is Damon?

At the faint chime of the elevator, my breath sticks in my throat as I pivot. But the sound of a heel striking marble has my hopes dashed.

Finley appears in the doorway. "Are you hungry?"

I blink at her several times before shaking my head. "No."

"Well, I am. You can keep me company, give me another lesson on how to have a conversation."

She spins to leave and I consider ignoring her. I could easily return to my room and shut the door. Say that I'm feeling sick. Or plead exhaustion. But my feet follow Finley's to the dining room.

"I asked Ms. Weathersby to make you soup." Finley points to a large covered urn and extends a bowl in my direction.

"Did Damon tell you to look after me?"

She puts the bowl back down, ignoring my question. "Eat what you want."

I exhale, rubbing at my forehead as Finley fills a plate with salad and chicken. She sets it down on the table with a loud *thunk* and drops into a chair.

I open the lid of the urn and sniff. Butternut squash with hints of cinnamon, allspice, and nutmeg. My favorite. I ladle a generous portion into a bowl and sit down opposite her. "I'm sorry, Finley. Thank you for being thoughtful." I take a taste and moan in appreciation, realizing I haven't eaten since yesterday.

"You looked ready to keel over downstairs. I figured you could do with a meal."

"It's not easy, adjusting to the fact that my life is a lie, that's for sure."

"Maybe it's not all bad."

I look up to find Finley's clear-eyed gaze on mine. "What do you mean?"

"Well, downstairs it seemed like you were able to make sense of things that didn't make sense to you before."

The soup is warm and comforting as it slides down my throat. The opposite effect of Finley's words. "Yes, things make sense now, but that doesn't mean any of this is okay. It's all so …" My voice trails off as I struggle to find words.

"Trashy?" Finley offers with a lifted brow.

"Fucked up," I counter, setting my spoon down.

"That too."

Before I realize what's happening, Finley and I are laughing. Not quiet, polite laughter. But big, loud belly laughs interspersed with tears and snorts.

And for a few moments at least, I forget that I don't know where Damon is or whether I can trust Finley.

chapter thirty-six

Damon

The not so muted hum of lively conversation coming from the dining room greets me when I arrive home. Without making my presence known, I listen for a few minutes.

I'm completely drained. The adrenaline rush of my time with Michael Clark has receded, exhaustion seeping into my bones. And yet, hearing Aislinn and Finley talking—laughing—puts a smile on my face. I back away, heading to my bedroom. Once there, I strip off the clothes I changed into barely half an hour ago.

I need another shower.

The sound of rushing water is eerily similar to the roar of the flames that consumed Michael's body. With each blink, I see an orange glow reflected on the backs of my eyelids, the acrid scent of burning flesh fills my nose, haunting my memories.

Again, I scrub my body with soap beneath a scalding spray. Not that it will do any good. My skin is permanently stained with the blood of so many men. Those I've killed myself, others who died on my orders.

I don't regret my actions, nor do I feel any guilt.

I haven't slayed any innocents.

Kill or be killed. That is my world.

It isn't a world I was born into, but it's the one I now inhabit.

A world I've chosen. A place I rule.

I've done what I've had to do.

Some may even call it poetic justice, ridding evil from the streets, one body at a time.

One day, I expect to die by another man's hands.

But not today.

Shutting off the water with an angry slam of the handle, I grab a towel. I run it over my head and face before wrapping it around my waist, reluctantly meeting my own eyes in the mirror. The truth blazing from them is inescapable, unavoidable.

Aislinn called me her savior—but she was wrong.

I am no savior. I am a savage.

And she saved herself.

Oh, she said Sebastián *let her go*. But I know that's not the full truth. Aislinn walked back through my door because she fought to get here.

Aislinn is a warrior princess.

She is my queen.

Most importantly, she is my wife.

And I will worship her—die for her—for as long as she'll have me.

Nothing less than forever.

A deep sigh rips through my chest and I put my hands on the counter, bowing my head.

I don't like what I heard about Chad Lytton today. He's become too close to Cruz for my comfort, and I will need to address it sooner rather than later.

I'm lost in my own thoughts when I feel a soft hand

sliding along my spine, a touch so light it's like being grazed by the wing of an angel.

"You're home." Aislinn's whisper is soft, almost breathy. Her words are marked by relief, edged in an exultant kind of joy I know I don't deserve.

Loving me is a curse, one I hope doesn't become a nightmare.

chapter thirty-seven

Aislinn

*D*uring a pause in conversation with Finley, I feel a tingling at the back of my neck, at the place where my spine meets my brainstem. The little hairs covering my skin stand up and flutter. There is only one person in the world whose mere presence provokes a physical response in me.

"Is Damon back?" I ask, wondering if she has the same sixth sense for him that I do.

But Finley merely shrugs and breaks off a piece from one of the oatmeal raisin cookies Ms. Weathersby brought in a few minutes ago, popping it in her mouth. "Nope. And unless he needs me, I'm going to eat this while it's still warm." She wrinkles her nose. "Because cold raisins, blech."

Her comment grabs my attention and prevents me from bolting off in search of Damon. "You only like raisins when they're warm?"

"Yep. Otherwise they're just like eating chewy bugs."

"Not even Raisinets?" I test her, suddenly fascinated. I've never met anyone else who won't eat cold raisins but loves them warm.

She mock gags. "Oh my God, those are the worst."

I take a bite of my own cookie and grin. The raisins are perfect. Plump and moist and not at all bug-like. "One of my friends used to bring those little red Sun-Maid boxes to school every day. I couldn't even watch her eat them without feeling queasy."

We finish eating, bring our plates into the kitchen, and thank Mrs. Weathersby. Before Finley heads for the elevator and I turn down the corridor toward Damon's private suite of rooms, I stop to give her a quick hug. She is stiff in my arms, but she doesn't push me away. "Thanks for checking up on me," I say, before releasing her.

"Ah, sure." Her lashes flutter as she breaks eye contact with me and jabs at the button. "See you around."

A bond is forming between Finley and me, one that could easily become friendship.

I really, really hope she's not the mole.

The sight of Damon's broad shoulders sends curls of warmth to slip around my ribs, squeezing the breath from my lungs. A white towel barely clings to his hips, droplets of water glistening against his tanned skin. I want to lick them. Lick him. Everywhere.

I manage to restrain myself, running the palm of my hand up his spine until I reach the swells of muscle supporting his neck, my fingernails disappearing into his dark hair. "You're home," I say.

Gratitude climbs up the back of my throat, forming a heavy knot I can barely swallow around. I have an urge to examine him, checking that he still has all his fingers and toes, that no one has hurt this man I don't ever want to live without.

He releases his hold on the counter, standing to his full height and turning to face me.

I gasp at the dark bruise in the center of his chest. It's not the kind he could have gotten from a stray punch or taking an elbow to the ribs. It looks like a major league ballplayer has thrown a fastball straight at the center of Damon's chest. And there is a deep gash bisecting his shoulder.

"What happened? Who did this to you?" Anger lends a raw timbre to my voice as I smooth gentle fingers over his mottled skin, a surge of concern and protectiveness heating my blood.

Yes, Damon is my big bad wolf, my devil, my dark knight. But most of all, he is mine.

And I am his.

I just wish I knew what that meant to Damon himself. Am I just a possession, or have I earned a place in his heart?

As he has in mine.

My brows pull together as I return my attention to his chest, then take a step back to scan the rest of his body. A few other scrapes and bruises. Rising to my tiptoes, I press a gentle kiss on his lips and another to the center of his chest before loosely wrapping my arms around his hips, taking care to rest my cheek against an unmarked patch of skin.

"I'm fine, princess," Damon murmurs. His deep sigh ruffles my hair as his hands come around to the small of my back, his chin finding purchase at the top of my head.

"No, you're not. Did Michael do this to you?" A single tear falls from the corner of my eye and I watch it slide over his skin until it is indistinguishable from the other droplets of water that cling to him.

He evades my question. "You won't have to worry about

him ever again."

I know what that means, and I cannot deny the relief that slips through my veins. "What about you?"

"What about me?"

"How often will I have to worry about you?"

I feel the vibration of his chuckle against my cheek before I hear it. "There's no need."

I'm not sure if it's because Damon is unaccustomed to anyone concerning themselves with his welfare, or if he's so convinced of his own invincibility that he can't believe anyone would doubt it.

Probably both.

"Don't tell me what to do," I say sternly. "And don't disappear on me again."

Damon drops a kiss on my forehead, his lips curved into a reluctant grin. "No more disappearing."

For some reason, I don't feel any relief at his pledge. If he were a little boy, I would check for crossed fingers. But Damon King is all man, and I have no reason to doubt he'll keep his word.

I drag my eyes to his face. "Does it hurt?"

The fire that burns behind his dark gaze is more intense than ever, though a grin pulls at a corner of his full lips. "Yes. Terribly. I think I need a distraction from the pain."

I blink up at him. "I'm not having sex with you—you need to go to a hospital. You probably need stitches."

He doesn't look at all concerned. "It's barely a graze. I'll be fine."

"And that bruise? You might have a broken rib."

"I've had worse."

I roll my eyes, going to the bathroom vanity and rifling through his drawers until I find gauze bandages and antibiotic ointment. I point to the bench in the corner of his bathroom. "Sit."

I rip open the bandage and dab a generous amount of ointment to the surface before laying it against Damon's shoulder and adhering the perimeter of the bandage to his skin. "You have to take it easy until this heals."

"Are you ordering me to bed?"

I concentrate on maintaining a stern expression. "I am. And there will be no funny business until you heal."

He arches a brow and stands up. "No laughing. I promise."

I squeal when he swings me into his arms, trying not to make contact with his chest or bandaged shoulder. "Damon, put me down. You can't, you shouldn't—"

He silences me with a kiss as he carries me into the bedroom, breaking away just long enough to mumble, "I can. And I am."

He would have. And I would have let him.

Except for the knock at the door.

He sets me down gently despite the murderous scowl on his face and stalks across the room, yanking at the knob. "Whatever it is—handle it."

Burke stands his ground. "Pretty sure you're going to want to deal with this yourself."

Damon's chin lifts, his chest expanding with an imminent denial.

But Burke speaks first. "Sebastián Cruz is here."

chapter thirty eight

Damon

"Get back in there and make sure the bastard doesn't leave."

I jog into my closet, dressing quickly in a white button-down shirt and charcoal trousers. Aislinn appears in the doorway as I'm buckling my belt. "Are you going to listen to what Seb has to say?"

Again with the *Seb*. "Like he consulted me before he took you?"

"He brought me back."

I step into my shoes and pin Aislinn with a stare burning from the frustration and fear I'd battled every minute of her absence. "You weren't his to take."

"I wasn't yours, either," she rebuts.

I step toward her until barely an inch separates our bodies, my height casting her face in shadow. "And now?"

Aislinn places her palms against my chest, not intimidated in the slightest by my size or my attitude. "I'm yours, Damon," she says. "But only because I want to be."

The caveman deep inside of me wants to pound on my chest and roar, lock Aislinn in this room while I break Cruz in two and send his sorry ass back to his father in Mexico. I feel my jaw working as my blood pressure soars. After a long moment, the surge of testosterone abates just enough to allow me to speak. "Fine. I won't kill him." *In front of you.*

"Well, I guess that's a start." There's a teasing note to her voice.

My eyes narrow. "Do you know why he's here?"

"No," she answers. "But I'd like to find out, don't you?"

I offer a begrudging nod even though the truth is: *Fuck, no.* The only thing I'd like to know is the sound his skull makes when it hits concrete after I toss him out the window. Let the Sanitation Department scrape him off the same sidewalk Aislinn was taken from.

But Aislinn has no idea about the thoughts running through my head, or the violent impulses simmering just beneath the surface of my skin, ready to erupt. "Promise you'll hear him out?"

Somehow, I manage another nod. "I'll let the fucker speak." *Before I break his jaw.*

She unclenches the fingers of my right hand that are already balled into a fist, entwining her fingers with mine. I allow it, knowing I can deliver just as powerful a punch with my left.

We walk into the corridor together to find Sebastián Cruz in my living room.

One of my men stands sentry in every corner, and Burke guards the entryway.

Cruz is near the fireplace, staring up at the painting. At our presence, he spins around. "You're a collector?"

I wave off the question. "What the fuck do you want?" The sight of him has cooled my blood, rendering my voice a quiet, steely monotone. The voice of an indifferent executioner.

"I hear congratulations are in order." My indifference

snaps the second his attention drifts to Aislinn. I have to grit my teeth against the urge to lunge for him. "I guess you made a more convincing argument than I did."

"It's not like that," Aislinn says, squeezing my hand.

Sebastián shrugs. "I don't need all the details of your arrangement. I'm here on business."

Good. Because this sure as fuck isn't a pleasure.

"If your last name wasn't Cruz, you would be dead by now."

"At whose hands, yours or my father's?"

"Whoever got to you first."

"Well, I'm not. My father tried doing things his way and he lost. You won, King. Los Muertos has lost too much money and too many men. I'm here to make a deal with you."

I like hearing this, but I'm not easily moved. "This coming from you or from him?"

"Both. Listen, Aislinn can tell you—I wanted out. I've never wanted to be a part of this world. My father's world, your world. If I had a choice, I'd be backpacking across Europe. Studying art, learning new languages, and staying the fuck out of New York and Mexico. But I don't have that option. So, the next best thing is to embrace my legacy and rebuild Los Muertos—my way. Not my father's."

I feel Aislinn's sharp inhale in the marrow of my bones. A quick glance at her face confirms her distress. I turn back to Sebastián. "That's why you're here? You steal my girl and now you're asking for my blessing to rebuild your territory—after I just tore it down?" Shit for brains.

"You really want the Albanians to take our place? New York will be the sex trafficking capital of the world in a year, tops."

"I've got that under control."

"Really—how? In a few months you'll have the

Colombians going after them. But the Colombians are sloppy, and they cut corners. You can't pay off enough politicians to cover up the spike in overdose deaths. So then you'll send the Russians in after them. And the Russians are going to want a slice of your crypto empire. You willing to give them a cut?"

I shift on my feet, not liking Sebastián's tone or the direction of this conversation. "My city, my problem," I bite out. Not liking that he's right.

"Sure it is." He tips his chin arrogantly. "And you're about to turn it into a war zone."

"Fuck off."

"If I leave, you're the one that's going to be fucked—"

I drop Aislinn's hands and step forward, plowing my right fist into the side of Sebastián's head and my left into the pit of his stomach. He counteracts with a surprisingly strong uppercut to my jaw.

The sound of a piercing whistle makes us both stop.

Aislinn pulls her fingers out of her mouth and puts her hands on her hips, staring at both of us accusingly.

"What the hell is wrong with the two of you? If you want to measure your dicks, I'll get you a ruler."

I take a reluctant step back, breathing heavily.

Sebastián points at me. "That first punch was deserved, but that's all you get. I'm here in good faith. My father has agreed to leave all operations based out of New York in my hands."

"If I agree to work with you."

He nods. "Yes."

"No." Aislinn's skin still has an angry flush. "If you want Damon to consider your offer, you need to come clean about everything. Give him the name of your father's spy."

I look from Aislinn to Sebastián and back again, keeping my face tight and mouth shut, unwilling to show weakness of any kind. "You heard her, Cruz."

Reluctance bleeds from his pores. "There is no spy. I was bluffing."

I don't want to believe that Los Muertos has managed to infiltrate my organization, but Cruz has backed down too easily. It doesn't sit right. "I don't work with liars."

Not true. I work with liars all day, every day. It's the nature of my business.

A vein pulses at Sebastián's temple as he stares unblinkingly. "I don't have a name. All I know is that it's a woman."

chapter thirty-nine

Aislinn

I feel my heart cracking. A woman. *Finley?*

Is her loyalty to Damon a lie?

Has she been using me for information against him?

Pretending to be my friend while stabbing me—and Damon—in the back?

I study Damon's expression as he absorbs Sebastián's admission. But his face shows absolutely nothing. It's a stunning landscape carved from granite. High, wide forehead. Strong, aristocratic nose bracketed by the diagonal slash of his cheekbones. The deep groove of his philtrum that leads to a generously sculpted mouth. Damon King is more beautiful than any piece of art I've ever seen. And here, in the fading light that shines through the windows, his brow furrowed in concentration, his lips a bold brushstroke of color over that sexy cleft chin, I want to know what is going on behind his stony facade.

What are you thinking, Damon? Are you hurting? Can I comfort you?

Will you let me?

The tension in the room is thick and impossible to ignore, surprise and dread keeping me rooted to the spot.

I can feel Sebastián's eyes on me, but I purposely don't look his way. My sole focus is Damon right now, the energy between us a visceral thing. Something in his stance, in the onyx glow of his eyes and throbbing vein that curves beneath his jaw, has me permanently entranced.

When Damon mutters an "excuse me" and stalks across the room for a quiet exchange with Burke, Sebastián appears at my side. "It's not too late," he whispers.

"For what?"

"We can still run away together. Away from all this."

Away from Damon.

Reading the pinched expression on my face, Sebastián adds, "Is this really the life you want, Aislinn? Do you love him enough to live a life you hate?"

I shake my head, feeling almost sorry for Sebastián that he doesn't understand the way I feel about Damon. The way I believe he feels about me. "Our relationship is … unusual. But Damon would never ask me to do something I believe is wrong. He respects me." Unlike the other men in my life.

But does he love me?

Damon returns, scowling at the closeness between Sebastián and me until we both take a step apart from each other. "If I let you run Los Muertos in my city," he finally says, "I'm going to ride your ass until I'm absolutely sure you're not just a straw man for your father."

"You can keep tabs all you want. I have my own agenda here."

"What makes you think your father's soldiers will give you their loyalty?"

Sebastián's answer comes smoothly. "Because they live here, in New York. They don't want a turf war with rival gangs and syndicates. They want to make fucking money."

"Hugo knows you're here?"

"Yes."

"And your brother?"

"Joaquin knows everything."

Damon's eyes narrow. "Tell me, who's really running the show? Your father or Joaquin?"

"Joaquin handles the day-to-day business of Los Muertos. My father gets involved in what interests him."

"Particularly your relationship status."

"Yes. Now that you and Aislinn are married, he's probably looking for some young virgin from the country." He shrugs. "You would think he was born in the eighteen hundreds."

"Did he arrange your brother's marriage too?" I ask.

Sebastián's face pinches tight. "I'm not sure, but Joaquin's wife died less than a year after their wedding. He hasn't remarried."

"I'm sorry," I say automatically, my voice soft.

He waves me off and turns back to Damon. "So, do we have a deal? You will rescind your orders to wipe out Los Muertos from the streets of New York?"

Damon counters, "In return for your continued cooperation and intel on any matter I deem of interest."

"Within reason."

"No. No stipulations."

Sebastián looks away for a moment, pushing out a heavy exhale. "Six months, King. You get six months of this, then we renegotiate."

"Fine. Because if you're not good for my city, you'll be out of here in less than that."

"Not going to happen."

"We'll see."

Sebastián grunts. "Now that Lytton's gone—"

"What do you mean gone?" I interrupt, my head swiveling

back to Damon. "Did you kill him?"

"No," he says quickly.

"He skipped town after your father informed him we would be married."

I bite the inside of my cheek, glaring at Sebastián. *After my father agreed to pimp me out like a prize broodmare.*

I don't mind that Chad's gone though. Maybe my father's next chief of staff will be a straight arrow and put an end to the corrupt practices of my father's administration. A girl can dream.

"You need someone on the inside, King. Someone who will—"

"Aislinn will do it."

My stomach clenches at Damon's quick answer, the air in my lungs evaporating at his utter disregard for my opinion. "No."

Sebastián's expression brightens. "Jesus Christ. It's brilliant."

"It would be just for a little while, until we get someone through the vetting process," Damon says, his stare a painful Taser that annihilates my equilibrium. "I'd like you to do it, for me."

"No," I repeat, my voice now a breathless rasp.

"It's the perfect solution," Sebastián adds.

"Exactly. No one will think twice about you stepping in as your father's chief of staff."

I look at Damon in utter shock. My belief in him, in *us*, has shattered.

A minute ago, I was telling Sebastián that Damon respected me. I was wrong.

"Perfect?" I shake my head vigorously. "It's far from perfect. And it's not happening."

chapter forty

Damon

*F*uck. That didn't go over well.

I hadn't planned on asking Aislinn to step in for Chad. But Sebastián was right. It made perfect sense.

Temporarily.

Once we found a suitable replacement, we'd leave on our honeymoon. Her stint as Granville's chief of staff would have been a distant memory by the time we arrived in the tropics.

But Cruz hadn't softened the blow at all and Aislinn stormed from the room, furious.

"Are you a fucking moron? Please tell me your people skills are better with Los Muertos soldiers, because when it comes to women, they suck."

Sebastián's brow lifts. "Like you're a ladies' man?"

No. Not anymore. I belong to exactly one lady … who hates me right now. "Fuck off." I pivot on my heel and catch Burke's eye. "Get him out of here before he causes me any more problems."

The sound of a slamming door to my right has me

heading back to my bedroom. "Aislinn?"

She doesn't answer, but I hear sounds coming from her closet. My stomach sinks when I get to the doorway. Aislinn is pulling clothes off their hangers and shoving them into a leather bag. "What the hell are you doing?"

"What does it look like? I'm leaving."

"For fuck's sake—again?"

She spins to face me. "This isn't like last time."

I shove my hands into my pockets and lean against the wall. "It sure as hell feels that way."

"I'll tell you what it feels like." Her eyes glitter with unshed tears. "It feels like manipulation. It feels like disillusionment. It feels like you don't give a shit about me, or anything I believe in."

"Because I asked you to step in as your father's chief of staff?"

"Yes!" Aislinn flings her hands into the air. "I'm not a cog in your greasy Tammany Hall political system."

"Fine. I asked, you said no. Let's move on."

Aislinn grabs another set of clothes. "That's what I'm doing."

"You're still packing."

"Because I'm still leaving."

I want to growl in frustration. "You've made your point. I get it."

The empty hangers she's holding drop to the floor. "No, you don't." Aislinn takes a few steps toward me before stopping herself, her chin trembling as she looks into my eyes. And for a moment, I think she sees whatever she needs to see. Reassurance. Comfort. Security. But then she blinks and the moment is gone. "I'm not running away because I'm mad at you. I'm leaving because you've shown me I have nothing to stay for."

I am stunned into silence, wanting that moment back.

That too-brief interlude when I thought our stand-off was at an end.

Instead we're at an altogether different end.

I have nothing to stay for.

The words reverberate inside my brain, beating against my eardrums.

"You can't leave!" I finally bellow, reaching for the only excuse that comes to mind. "We're married."

"I can, and I am," she snaps. "Honestly, I don't know what I was thinking. Being with you is like jumping from the frying pan into the fire. I quit my job when I realized what kind of organization my father was running when he and Chad expected me to help them. And now you're doing the same damn thing."

"Just hear me out."

"No." She shakes her head. "I won't. And you won't sweet talk me into changing my mind, either."

Shock flows through my veins as I watch Aislinn throwing shoes into a shopping bag. "So, that's it … You're just going to leave me?"

"I'm not in danger anymore, right?"

"You still need to take precautions—"

"But I'm not about to be grabbed off the streets."

"No." It is a very reluctant admission.

"Good. I'm going to check into a hotel and take some time to figure my life out."

"I own six apartment buildings. You can have your choice of—"

She whirls around, her eyes blazing. "Exactly. *My* choice, Damon. Whether I decide to stay in a hotel or a park bench is up to me."

Park bench, my ass. "Fine." I lift my hands, palms out. "Stay where you want."

She makes a discontented noise and turns away from me.

But I'm not through, and I won't be dismissed. "Fuck working in the DA's office. Where does this leave us?"

Aislinn doesn't stop moving, but she does slow down, her shoulders drooping. I push off the wall and close the space between us, wrapping my arms around her waist and pulling her into me. I press my nose into her tousled blonde crown, breathing deep. Aislinn's honeyed sweetness expands within my lungs, filling my chest cavity, engulfing me in her light.

How the fuck am I ever going to let this girl go? How?

Every cell in my body gives a vicious protest at the thought.

I don't want to.

I don't want to.

I don't want to.

Ever.

But I should.

What can I offer Aislinn?

Crime and corruption. Dirty Politics. Dangerous threats.

No. I will not be the warden who imprisons her within a cage she doesn't deserve.

Not again.

Not ever again.

"Damon, I'm leaving."

Her whisper creates a gaping chasm in the marrow of my bones. I know I need to let her go.

But I don't.

I spin her around and draw her back against my chest. I push my fingers into her thick mane and gather the silken strands into a fist, tugging on them until Aislinn moans. "I know." I release a shuddering exhale. "But not yet."

Aislinn leans back into the grip of my hand, her eyes meeting mine. Gleaming with unshed tears, they are deep pools of need. The warmth of Aislinn's breath caresses my throat, loosening the heavy knot of bitterness lodged there.

Lifting Aislinn by her waist, I set her down on the marble counter, her thighs parting to span my hips.

I can taste Aislinn's sweetness before our lips meet. A coarse groan rumbles from my chest as I slide my lips over hers. Once. Twice. The lightest of passes. Not quite a kiss, not nearly a claiming.

Is this what surrender feels like?

Mob bosses, cartel leaders, crooked politicians. They are mere pawns on my chessboard.

For a chance at forever with Aislinn, I'd upend the game entirely.

Except that my sins are too many, my enemies too merciless. Forever is impossible.

Our mouths finally fuse together, Aislinn's moan a vibration that makes something deep in the pit of my belly clench hard. As I run my tongue along the seam of her lips, I untuck fabric from the hem of her skirt, her lips opening as I tug at the buttons running down her chest and push the silk over her shoulders.

Fuck. I pull back just enough to take her in. Smooth ivory skin. That perfect pink temptation of a mouth. The golden strands scattered across her shoulders, sliding over her collarbone. The sweep of inky black lashes framing twin pools of the deepest, purest blue.

Aislinn's beauty is the reason poems are written, songs are sung, painters are inspired to put brush to canvas. It's elegant and subtle. Quietly obvious, completely undeniable.

When our lips meet again, I unclasp the band of her bra and run my hands over the satin expanse of her back, my fingertips tracing each disc of her spine, the delicate wings of her shoulder blades. There is no part of her I don't want to touch and taste. Admire and adore. Forever.

I can feel Aislinn's temperature rising, the heat emanating from between her thighs. She is so light, her waist so narrow as I pull her off the countertop and set her on her feet. The zipper of her skirt makes a whine of protest the moment before it is just a puddle of black fabric on the floor. Her lace thong follows.

I pull Aislinn into my arms. Her thighs wrap around me, her ankles crossing just below my ass. I curse, feeling her slick heat against my skin. "You're so fucking wet for me."

A soft sigh tumbles from her mouth as she tucks her head beneath my chin. "You have that effect on me."

I grunt as I sit down on the wide bench set against one of the walls, positioning Aislinn over my lap. "Do you remember your first night here?"

She gives a little sigh of pleasure as my hands roam over the smooth swells of her ass, the silky stretch of her thighs. "It was pretty unforgettable."

"Your ass was bright pink from your fall."

"Mmm. Don't remind m—"

Her words are cut off by the loud slap of my palm striking her skin. A fresh surge of anger fills my chest as I recall the danger she'd knowingly put herself in that night. Anger at myself for creating a situation where she would risk lighting a fire in a locked room.

Anger that this will be our last night together.

Aislinn gasps, but she doesn't struggle. My hand falls, again and again. I am methodical in this overdue punishment, soothing her skin between slaps, running my hand between her trembling thighs, sliding my fingers inside that pink pussy that's swollen and glistening, taunting me with each jerk of Aislinn's hips.

I thrust inside her wet heat, my movements deep and forceful. "I took care of you then. And I'll take care of you now." Another slap, another gasp, another caress and thrust.

Aislinn moans into the upholstered cushion, her small hands bunching the fabric into her fists as she squirms against my thighs.

By the time I even consider stopping, Aislinn's ass is as shiny pink as a summer sunset. I let my hand fall one more time before leaning down to blow cool air over her stinging skin. She trembles, a keening cry escaping her mouth. "Sh," I whisper, gathering her into my arms and holding her close to me.

Aislinn's cheeks are wet, her lashes black spikes that flutter against my neck as she hiccups and pants. I wait a minute before picking her up in my arms and changing positions. "You won't forget tonight, either," I say quietly, more to myself than to her as I lay her across the bench and quickly get undressed.

As I straddle her, I read the questions in her eyes and press a kiss onto her lips before she can ask them. Tonight is not for talking.

Tonight is for touching and tasting and fucking. Licking and sucking and thrusting.

And maybe … maybe even loving.

My mouth on Aislinn's is firm and fierce, swallowing down the doubts and questions I know she must have. Only when I feel her hips buck against me do I slide my lips down the curve of her jaw, exploring the downy sweet skin of her neck and the sensitive skin tucked behind the curve of her ear.

I push fingers that are still slick from Aislinn's pussy past her lips. She makes a wanton sound in the back of her throat, her tongue lapping furiously.

Meanwhile, I press my tongue into the fluttering hollow between her collarbone, lingering over the pulse point for a moment before licking down to her breasts. I suck at her peaked nipples, my tongue sweeping over the ripe areolas that have turned dusky with desire, then the plump underside that curves into the fretted plane of her ribs. I mark my path to her navel with bite marks, shallow impressions that will only remain on her skin temporarily.

Except that I want to fucking brand this woman. Send her away with a mark of ownership forever emblazoned on her skin. Proof that she is mine, will always be mine.

Mine. I growl as I swirl my tongue inside her belly button, then move lower. Another nip on each of her hip bones, more on her inner thighs. My tongue delves into the hollows behind her knees, feasts on the fleshy part of her calves. I suck Aislinn's toes into my mouth, pressing a hand flat against her belly as she wriggles and shrieks before flipping her over and making a similar exploration of her still glowing ass, the narrow curve of her waist, and the straight ladder of her spine.

I suck on her neck and run my nose through the long, golden strands of her tousled mane, inhaling deeply. Never again will I massage shampoo into this hair until it is a thick, slippery mass, rinsing suds from every strand until they cascade down her back like a waterfall of molten bronze.

My deep, regretful groan ruffles her hair and Aislinn rolls over, cupping her palms over my cheeks and kissing me again. Our tongues twist and writhe inside our mouths, her breath filling my lungs, my breath filling hers. My mind finally quiets as I am filled with the scent and taste of Aislinn. Her legs wrap around my waist, her fingers lacing together behind my neck as I brace myself on my forearms above her, my knees on either side of her hips. There is nothing between us except for my cock, pulsing and pressing into the flat expanse of her belly.

It would be so easy to pierce her right now. A slight shift upward, a smooth movement forward. But I haven't tasted the deepest, most intimate, part of her yet today. I haven't felt her buck and shiver, the sound of my name on her lips muffled by the grip of her thighs as they clench against my ears.

Before I can be deterred, I pull away and slide downward, ignoring Aislinn's moan of protest.

Spreading her thighs, I take a moment to appreciate the bounty spread before me. The pale pink of her outer lips, the darker, glistening folds within, topped by the swollen nub of her clit that practically begs for my attention, the seam that leads to the tiny, puckered hole that expands just enough to grant me access.

My tongue explores every inch and crevice, savoring the taste of her. There is a hint of earthiness to Aislinn's sweetness that is intoxicating. I gorge myself, licking and sucking and eating until Aislinn thrashes beneath my face, until the tremors rolling through her body finally cease and her hands pull at my hair, her thighs finally dropping away from my neck.

I rise, rubbing my cheeks over Aislinn's breasts, coating them with her wetness before kissing her again, sharing the taste of her that still coats my lips and tongue as I drag the head of my cock through her slit. For a long minute, or maybe an hour, that's all I do.

Kiss and tease.

Kiss and tease.

Until the throbbing becomes almost painful and I can't take another second without being inside her.

The tight clench of Aislinn's pussy feels like home, and I don't hold back the growl of possession that rumbles from my throat. I stare down at her, committing to memory the blissful smile that pulls at her kiss-swollen lips, the flush of her skin made even more so by the abrasions from my stubbled jaw, her pupils so dilated by desire that only a smudge of blue is visible.

"Damon," she whispers. Her voice is thick with wonder; a tremulous gasp.

I smile at Aislinn, positioning her so she's straddled over my hips. "Say my name again, princess."

"Damon," she repeats, leaning forward and placing her hands at my shoulders as she begins to ride me. This is usually one of my least favorite positions, but not tonight. Aislinn's alabaster skin glows, her soft lines and lush curves carved by the deft hand of a master, the swells of her breasts bouncing in the most enticing way.

I hold her hips, guiding her motions as she rises and falls, fascinated by the emotions that cross her face. Determination. Desperation. Desire.

Aislinn's movements grow frenzied and jerky, her mouth falling open as her eyes close. Another orgasm so close.

I am close, too. I could fucking come just from watching Aislinn riding me. I press my thumb against Aislinn's clit at the same time as I pull her down to me. The friction sends us both flying over the edge and I swallow her exultant shriek with another kiss.

Nothing tastes as good as Aislinn.

And nothing will hurt as bad as goodbye.

chapter forty-one

Aislinn

*D*amon falls asleep before I do. At least, I think he does. I'm not sure that he ever allows himself to be completely at ease. There's always a tension to Damon's muscles, an intensity in his expression. I have a sense that his mind is never entirely quiet. That he's planning and scheming even in his dreams.

Right now, his breaths are peaceful but his arms around me haven't loosened. He holds me tightly as if he's afraid I will try to escape in the middle of the night.

I won't.

Not yet.

I'm too tired. Exhausted, physically and emotionally. And not from sex. Well, not just from sex.

Sex. Somehow, that three letter word doesn't seem nearly big enough to define what just happened. How, at first, his lips merely hovered over mine, breathing me in like I was something precious, a rare piece of art for him to worship. Like even my kisses were meant to be savored. And then, when he finally allowed his mouth to cover mine, he latched on with a hunger that swept me away. I was plunged into a deep, fast moving current that felt vast and powerful—and yet intensely intimate. As if Damon and I had an entire ocean to ourselves.

Every bit of resentment, every fear and doubt and question weighing so heavily on me ... they all sunk to the bottom. There was only the two of us. His body. My body. Our kisses.

I would call it making love, except that I hate that term. I've always hated it. It belongs to women holding a martini in one hand and a cigarette in the other, punctuating their sentences with *dahling*.

Besides, Damon still hasn't said the L-word.

And when Damon picked me up and carried me to bed, pulling me close, I lifted his hand to my face and dropped a breathless kiss on his knuckles. "This doesn't change anything," I whispered, the words scraping my tongue like jagged blades of broken glass.

He had stiffened, remaining quiet.

I almost turned over, so that I could look into Damon's eyes. But I hadn't. Painful truths are easier to bear when I can close my eyes and pretend I'm whispering into the dark.

Eventually, Damon pressed a lingering kiss onto the top of my head, his softly spoken, "I know," ruffling my hair and sending a spray of goose bumps down my arms.

My pillow is damp when I wake up. As if I've cried a thousand tears during the night.

The swollen, red-rimmed eyes that greet me in the mirror

confirm it.

Surprisingly, more fall when I walk into the closet, reminders of our passion slapping me in the face. The bag of clothes that was pushed to the floor when Damon lifted me onto the island. The oversized upholstered bench we'd used like a mattress. The smell of sex that still lingers in the air.

I dress quickly and gather as many of my things as I can carry. I don't worry that Damon will stop me. Last night had been more than just sex. It was the end of our story. It was goodbye.

Which is why I twist the gorgeous ring off my finger and place it in the center of the granite countertop. The canary diamond flashes brightly beneath the crystal chandelier. Glints of gold that sear my corneas and raze my skin.

Goodbye, husband.

The men in the hall offer to help with my bags, but I only shake my head. I welcome their weight, the pinch of the straps digging into my shoulders. I need to feel something, anything, other than heartache.

I throw myself into the back of the car, mumbling the name of the hotel I booked this morning from my phone. Each breath is a struggle. My lungs feel like they can't inflate properly, my brittle ribs protesting with each attempted inhale.

Before we pull away from the curb, the door opens. And for a brief moment, there is no more pain. A flash of euphoria explodes inside my brain, glitter made of rainbows and unicorns and pure, unfiltered happiness drenching me like rain.

But it's not Damon.

"Finley." Euphoria deteriorates into sharp shards of disappointment and confusion.

The car merges into traffic and she asks, "Where are we going?"

"A hotel, for now." Where I'm going to watch the most depressing movies ever made, order comfort food from room service, and raid the minibar. Not necessarily in that order.

"What about your parents—you're not staying with them?"

"I'll see my mom, but I think I'm going to steer clear of my father for a while."

"And Damon?"

"Him, too."

For a long moment, neither of us says anything. I let my eyes drift to the window. So many people in this city. Everyone living their own lives, consumed by their own problems. It's entirely possible that I will never see Damon King again.

Outside, buildings fly by, one after the other. Steel skyscrapers and brick brownstones, corporate office buildings and luxury high-rises. Men strutting in suits, women striding in stilettos. Joggers darting around nannies pushing strollers.

Life rolls on.

"What about me?" The question is softly spoken.

When I turn to face her, Finley blinks and averts her eyes. "What do you mean?"

After a small sigh, she reluctantly meets my gaze. "Are you leaving me behind, too?" Discomfort is etched into her pursed lips and narrowed eyes. I can see how hard it is for Findley to ask the question.

I hesitate from surprise, not reluctance. "No," I answer after a long moment. Because one side of my brain acknowledges the tentative beginnings of a friendship between us, and I don't want to throw that away.

Meanwhile, the political strategist side of me knows it's a smart idea. *Keep your friends close and your enemies closer.* I can't forget that someone in Damon's organization—*a woman*—is still a threat. A woman that could very well be my new friend.

Finley holds my stare and then finally nods. "Forget the hotel," she says loudly, directing her voice at the driver. "We're going to my place."

"What—"

"I work all the time, you can have it mostly to yourself. Figure out what you want to do with your life. And every once in a while, we can have dinner together. Or whatever."

Her words are a spontaneous jumble and I look at her curiously. "Did Damon put you up to this?"

"No. But girlfriends are supposed to be there for each other, especially after a breakup." She shrugs, her fingers drumming against her thighs. "I don't really know from personal experience or anything but that's what seems to happen in every rom-com, anyway."

"You watch rom-coms?" I ask, a brow edging upward.

She picks at an invisible piece of lint along her inseam. "Maybe."

I cover her hand with one of my own, putting a stop to her nervous fidgeting. "Thank you. I'd like that. Just—please tell me you have ice cream." Her brows lift. "And vodka. Or tequila. Alcohol of some kind."

Keep your friends close and your enemies closer.

It's time to find out if Finley is a friend or foe.

chapter forty two

Damon

I need a drink. Whiskey, neat. Times ten.

A priest. An exorcism.

A brain surgeon. A lobotomy.

Someone—some *way*—to erase the memory of Aislinn from my mind, her honeyed scent from my olfactory senses, the sweet tartness of her pussy from my taste buds.

Expunge the feel of her velvety smooth skin, the gentle rise of her curves, the tight, wet clench of her around my cock.

Eradicate the spun gold of her hair and the deep ocean blue of her eyes from my corneas.

Obliterate the twinkling sound of her laugh and her desperate, needy moans from my ears.

Of course, there is more to Aislinn Granville than my five senses can absorb. There is the bristling fierceness of her personality as she challenges my authority. The unwavering loyalty she exhibits to those she loves. The wide streak of courage that runs through her like a steel beam.

And I want all of it—all of *her*—gone.

Gone.

Except I don't. Not really.

Fuck. Not at all.

I want her fucking back. In my life. In my apartment.

In my arms.

And, I swear to fucking God, I will never let her go again.

But that emotion, that unbridled *need*, is exactly what I am desperate to avoid.

I should know—I led with my emotions once before. I allowed my heart to override my head when I sought revenge on my stepfather. The result: I was sent to jail and my mother wound up in the morgue.

I will not make the same mistake again.

I will approach this situation as if it's a goddamn business school case study. Facts. Data. Details.

I cannot think about Aislinn as a person I lo—

My mind slams shut like a trapdoor on the four-letter word. *Love.* It is as welcome in my world as a bout of polio.

Love is weakness.

Obviously.

It's been a week since Aislinn left, and she took my strength with her.

Because I'm a mess. An unfocused, unmotivated mess.

Just like Granville. Without his daughter to use as his personal pawn, he is a mess too. Lytton's absence has plunged his office into chaos.

Which has actually worked out just fine for me.

I have also managed to scrutinize every single one of my employees, male and female. Which only further confirmed that Sebastián Cruz was bullshitting me about a goddamn mole. *Dick.*

"What?" I snap at Burke when he pokes his head around the door to my office. He doesn't react; this is my new normal.

"Davina sent details on—"

"You and Finley can handle it."

"She's not here."

"Where the fuck is—"

But I stop myself mid-growl. Finley is with Aislinn. She's been spending a lot of time with Aislinn lately. A lot of time that she's not here.

I wish I could pretend that the viscous stew churning inside my gut is anger.

But it's not, and lying to myself won't make it so.

It's jealousy, plain and simple.

"Fine." I spin my chair around and turn my attention to the file Davina uploaded to our server. Another victim. Another abusive asshole. Three young kids. The report includes hospital reports, audio files of 911 calls, financial details, her own observations. "Christ," I mutter, catching a note about the twelve-year-old daughter receiving treatment for gonorrhea. She refused to name her father as her rapist, but since the mother received treatment for the same strain, it is obvious.

"Yeah. This is a bad one."

"Why the fuck isn't this guy in jail?"

"He's a cop."

I let out a stream of unintelligible curses. "Where are the mother and kids?"

"Davina got 'em out this morning. They're in one of our apartments for now, but we need to move fast with them."

"Gimme a couple of hours to work on the financials. Do we have new IDs?"

"Yeah, Finley took care of it before she left."

"You're keeping track of the husband?"

"He's working a shift right now. I talked to a contact in his precinct and he's going to be assigned overtime."

"How long?"

"As long as we need."

I nod. "I'll let you know when things are taken care of on my end."

Burke throws me a bloodthirsty leer. "You'll feel better once this scum isn't breathing."

I won't. But if I do, it will only be fleeting.

I don't even want to feel better. Wallowing in misery is preferable.

I lost the only good thing in my life. My bright light. My sunshine. My spitfire.

My goddess. My queen.

I'd forfeit my empire to get Aislinn back.

That is, if I deserved her.

But I don't. She's better off without me.

I might be a corrupt motherfucker, but I will not tarnish the shiny jewel that is Aislinn Granville.

Technically, Aislinn King.

She is still my wife.

Neither of us have severed the connection that now exists only on paper.

Groaning, I hack into the asshole's bank accounts. Even if we kill him, it will be easier if all assets are transferred to his wife's new identity. His kids shouldn't have to stand by their father's grave, crying any more tears over the man that caused them so much pain. Let them start a new life somewhere, have a fresh start.

That's what Aislinn deserves too. She left her ring behind, along with the cell phone and laptop I gave her. I'm not tracking her movements anymore. Could I find out if she got a new phone, a new computer, a new apartment? Yes. Could I track her credit card and social media activity? Yes.

I could.

But I don't.

For the first time in over a decade, I have no idea what

Aislinn is doing or where she is going. Finley swore that she would keep an eye on Aislinn, not because I asked her to, and I am trusting her.

It's driving me insane.

chapter forty three

Aislinn

"I'm home!" Finley's voice echoes throughout her Lower East Side loft. According to her, the building was an old factory that had been managed by a slumlord and left to rot. Finley bought it from foreclosure, renovated it, and now has the entire top floor to herself.

I haven't yet decided whether her refusal to live in one of Damon's buildings is suspicious, or just fitting with her independent nature.

"Hey." I lift my hand from the depths of her oversized sectional and wave. It's where I've spent most of the day. Most of every day for the week I've been here.

I roll out of bed in the morning, spend an hour or two with my mother, who may or may not acknowledge my presence, change back into sweats and am couch-surfing by noon.

"Are you hungry? Mrs. Weathersby was taking a batch of oatmeal raisin right out of the oven just before I left. The raisins are still warm."

My nose twitches at the scent of cinnamon and sugar, but

my stomach twists in protest. "No, thanks." My diet is primarily ice cream washed down with vodka these days. I wouldn't recommend it.

But Finley plops down beside me and pushes a cookie at my face anyway. "Eat this. We need to talk."

I take it reluctantly, biting off a small piece. "What's wrong?"

"You."

"Me?"

"Yes. A few nights of moping on the couch and watching sappy movies is more than enough."

I cough on a fleck of oatmeal. "Fine. I'll get out of your hair."

Finley rolls her eyes and tosses a black leather bag in my lap.

"What's this?"

"It's your get out of jail card."

I frown in confusion, setting the cookie I didn't want on the end table. "What are you talking about?"

"In there is everything you need to start a new life. New identity. Plenty of cash. Login code to a bank account with enough money to set you up for life—anywhere in the world."

I pull open the zipper in shocked silence, quickly discovering physical proof of Finley's statement. "Why are you giving this to me?"

"You were leaving when Cruz's men took you. I'm just giving you what you want."

That morning I walked out of Damon's apartment ... I just wanted some space. Some room to breathe.

"I live here," I insist. "My life is here."

She snorts. "Really? That's what you call it?"

The truth hurts. And so does Finley's exasperated delivery. "I—"

Before I can continue, she exhales and falls back against the couch cushions. "I'm sorry. I just … I hate watching you disintegrate like this. What happened to the woman who started a fire in a locked room?"

"She was a stupid girl," I mumble.

"No. She was brave enough to go after what she wanted. And strong enough to take risks. I liked that woman. More importantly, I respected her."

"No, you didn't. You hated her." Strangely, talking about myself in the third person doesn't feel wrong. Because I feel completely disconnected from the person I was. I am split into two.

"I wanted to *be* her, Aislinn," Finley says, shaking her head. "My sister, the badass."

If I was surprised by the bag on my lap, I am floored by what I just heard. I pause for a moment. "Your … *what?*"

"You heard me."

"But—I don't understand."

"Ace is my father, too."

From the time I was old enough to sit on Santa's lap until I outgrew the holiday tradition altogether, there was only one thing I ever truly wanted. Sure, I asked for various dolls and toys. But at the top of every list, my most fervent wish—a sister.

My mother would take the piece of paper from my hands with a wobbly smile. *I'll send this to the North Pole right away.*

On Christmas morning there would be toys and candy and clothes. But never a sister.

I must have been the only little girl who didn't like Santa Claus.

And now, after all this time, to discover I have a sister …

I'm heartbroken.

And angry.

And hurt.

Not just because Finley clearly wants me to leave. But that she doesn't want to get to know me. Not now, not then.

"How long have you known?"

"A while."

"A while as in days? Weeks? Years?" My voice rises an octave with each word.

"Years," Finley admits.

"You've known about me for years?" I squeak. "Am I so awful that you didn't want to meet me—you didn't care at all?" Another thought occurs to me and I cover my gasp with my palm, speaking through my fingers. "Do I have another sister or brother? Were you an only child?"

"It's just us, as far as I know." She looks almost sheepish. "And we did meet, although I didn't know about our connection until years afterward."

Years. So much time, wasted. And now, so many questions. I tear my eyes away from Finley for a moment—eyes that are identical to mine—needing to gather my thoughts. My mother. Finley's father ... Ace. My father.

I pause for a moment before asking, "What was he like?"

"Ace?"

I jerk my chin in a shallow nod.

"I was only ten when he went to prison. But he used to walk me to school in the morning. And every Wednesday he would pick me up from school and take me to dance class, and then for ice cream." Her eyes lift and she gives me a sad smile.

"Really? My mom did the same with me." I tilt my head at the odd coincidence. "That's so strange. Mrs. Br—"

"—early's Dance Studio." There's no surprise on Finley' face.

I'm dumbfounded. "You think—you think they planned it?"

"I know they did. It was how Ace got to see you."

"I—I never noticed."

Finley leans back. "I know."

For several beats, neither of us say anything. "I hated those damn dance classes," she says eventually.

"Really? I loved them."

"Of course, you did," Finley says sarcastically. "You came in with a different tutu every week, and you didn't trip over your feet every other eight-count."

"So," I clear my throat, "why didn't you want to get to know me?"

"When Ace went to jail, I was stuck with my con artist mother. Dragged along from mark to mark. Meanwhile, you lived a life of wealth and privilege. What would you want with me?"

I gape at her. "I'd have wanted exactly what I want right now. To get to know you. You're my family."

"We share a few strands of DNA. You don't owe me anything."

I lift the bag on my lap. "And this is what you owe me?"

"The chance to be that brave, strong girl again?" She exhales a frustrated sigh. "Yeah, I do."

I open the passport cover to find my face and a stranger's name. "Amy Reynolds, fleeing the country like a refugee, is that girl?"

"There's a plane waiting for you at Teterboro. You can go wherever you want, start over somewhere else."

It's impossible to ignore the irony of this moment. How many times in the past month have I wished I could leave this city behind and never look back? Forget about Damon, my father, Chad, Sebastián. Remember my mother as she was, and not the shell of a person she is now.

A fresh start. It's what I wanted.

But is it what I want?

Damon King.

His name flashes in my mind.

He is what I want. My devil. My dark knight. My forever.

Finley reads it in my face and groans. "Seriously, Aislinn. Don't be the girl who can't figure her own shit out. There's more to life than dick. What do *you* want? Who do *you* want to be?"

My mind grinds to a halt in protest, my thoughts becoming sluggish. But Finley doesn't make any attempt to hurry me. "The Network," I finally say. "I want to continue my work with The Network."

"Well, have you reached out to Davina?"

"No. I've been busy."

"Busy?"

"Busy wallowing in self-pity," I admit.

"You done now?"

My head dips forward in a shaky nod. "Yes. I think I am."

"Finally." She rolls her eyes. "I don't know which of you is more pathetic. Damon's a goddamn mess, too."

It's the first time she's mentioned him since I've been staying with her, both of us creeping around his name like it's a curse.

She picks up what's left of my cookie and stands. "Waste of perfectly warm raisins," she grumbles. "I'm going to head back to work. Should I tell the pilot to get the plane ready?"

I pick up the bag from my lap and return it to Finley. "No. I won't be needing it."

chapter forty four

Aislinn

*H*alf an hour after Finley leaves, I am out the door myself.

I needed a kick in the ass and she gave me one.

Along with a dose of reality.

I have reasons to stay in New York.

A sister.

The Network.

And the man I love.

I don't want to talk about myself in the third person. I don't want to feel disconnected and ashamed of who I've become.

It's time for me to put on my big girl panties and woman-up. The spitfire is back.

First, I buy myself my own phone and laptop to replace the ones I left behind. Next, I call Davina.

"Aislinn, is that you?"

"Yes. Sorry, it's been so long." And I am sorry. I forgot how important The Network is to me. How important our work is to those who need it.

"We all need a break sometimes. How are you doing?"

"I'm good." I pause. "Well, I'm getting there. Which is actually why I'm calling—"

"You know what?" Davina interrupts. "Let's have this conversation in person. Are you free for dinner?"

"Yes," I answer quickly, my appetite suddenly reappearing after a week-long hiatus. "Where should I meet you?"

She names a restaurant I'm familiar with and we agree to meet in an hour. I hurry back to Finley's apartment, drop off my heavy shopping bag, and start walking uptown. I could take a cab, but the fresh air feels good. Well, as fresh as Manhattan air can get. I've been cooped up for so long, physically and mentally.

As I begin walking uptown, I call a real estate agent I've worked with in the past. I explain what I'm looking for and she agrees to send me a few potential listings. We make tentative plans to meet up tomorrow.

I know I should probably call a headhunter, but I'm in no rush to get back to politics just yet.

I reach the restaurant a few minutes early and order a tea. Davina arrives just as I'm taking my first sip. She kisses me on both cheeks and pulls me into a warm embrace. I linger for longer than I normally would have, and when we pull apart, I am blinking back tears.

She slides in across from me, glances at my tea and says to the server, "I think we need something stronger. Two Belvedere martinis. Straight up, with a twist."

I break into a laugh. "It's been that kind of day?"

"Frankly, yes. How about you?"

"It's been that kind of week. Month." I push my teacup and saucer aside. "But things are looking up."

She smiles. "I'm glad to hear that." She lowers her voice. "Are you ready to come back to work again?"

"I am." The waiter returns with two chilled martini

glasses, pouring them directly from the cocktail shaker. We clink glasses and I take a grateful sip. "I'd also like to become more involved in your charity work and advocacy efforts. I believe I can be of value, given my political background. I understand the issues involved and am a passionate advocate for domestic violence survivors. If you will consider—"

Davina stops me by covering my hand with one of her own. "Yes."

"Yes?"

"Yes. You are a capable, courageous woman. I would be honored to work with you."

The warmth that fills me isn't from the vodka. I return her grin. "Thank you, Davina. That means the world to me. I was worried my situation would have changed things."

"What situation?"

I hesitate for a moment. "Damon and me. We were together for a hot minute and now we're not. I thought you might ..."

My voice trails off and Davina intervenes. "The women and children who need our help take precedence over personal drama, always."

I breathe a sigh of relief and take another sip. The vodka is a cool, bracing splash over my tongue. "Yes, of course."

She spends a few minutes talking, in vague terms, about the newest package that needs to be delivered outside of New York. It's obvious that this work takes a toll on Davina. The responsibility isn't an easy burden to bear, and their stories weigh on the soul. "I'm going to check on them after leaving here, would you like to join me?"

"Absolutely." I've only had brief interactions with the people we help, and I know it's significant that Davina has asked me to join her tonight.

We order our meal, and over dinner we discuss upcoming legislation affecting abused women and children, a grant

Davina would like to apply for, and some new advocacy work I might be interested in pursuing. It is after the check has been paid that she asks, "So, where do things stand with you and Damon right now?"

"I don't know," I answer with a dejected shake of my head. "I don't think I can live in his world. What he does goes against everything I believe in."

"Everything? Do you know how many women and children would be dead right now, or living lives of shame and abuse?" Her voice is gentle, but each word lands with the force of a mallet striking bone.

"Of course. That's not what I object to. It's … everything else," I finish lamely.

"And you don't love him enough to attempt a compromise?"

A knee-jerk denial turns to dust before it leaves my mouth. Instead, I say, "I'm not sure if it's enough."

"You know, Aislinn, I've seen love twisted in too many unrecognizable ways. Love is used as a weapon, a threat, an excuse, a defense." She pats my shoulder, staring into my eyes. "That said, when it's true, it's worth fighting for."

chapter forty five

Damon

We are born with two hundred and seventy bones. As we age, some fuse together so that by the time we are adults, we have two hundred and six. Theoretically, you can break almost all of them without actually dying. But in reality, your body will go into shock sooner rather than later.

This cop has a file nearly as long as most criminals. He's been written up for excessive force, coerced confessions, racial profiling, tardiness, drinking on the job, unwarranted search and seizures, insubordination ... And the list of every injury sustained by his wife and children—every reported injury, that is—is even longer.

The beating Burke and I mete out is methodical and precise, designed to inflict maximum pain. I don't feel even the tiniest shred of remorse as his ribs crack beneath the force of my fist. Not when blood streams from his face and ears and my cracked knuckles. Not when his screams and pleas become unintelligible because his teeth are just bloody shards scattered on the ground.

Like the cold-blooded killer I am, I feel nothing.

Later, after a shower, I decide to visit the people I did it for. Hoping that something, anything, will penetrate this fog I'm in.

The fog that has become my home since Aislinn left.

Unannounced visits to those who have been living in terror are best avoided, so I text Davina to say that I will be stopping by.

I knock once and then use my key to enter. Davina is sitting with the wife, no doubt going over their escape itinerary.

I sense Aislinn before I see her. It is the faint sweetness that perfumes the air, the heightened energy that makes my heartbeat kick up a notch, the almost imperceptible lightening of my steps. My eyes are drawn toward the window. Aislinn is sitting on the floor, bookended by a girl coloring in a sketchpad and a boy peering at what looks like an instruction book to a Lego set. The other daughter is sitting on the couch nearby, reading a book.

Aislinn looks up, swatting at the molten river of blonde impeding her vision. Instantly, her full lips curve into a grin, her blue eyes beaming with happiness. But just as quickly as her joyful expression appears, it is gone.

Leaving me wondering if it had ever been there at all.

I blink, and Aislinn is wearing an aloof mask. The ice princess I remember well. The ice princess that set fire to more than just a bed.

She built a blaze that consumed my willpower, my ambitions, my heart.

I cross the room. "Legos, huh?"

The little boy peers up at me. "We're trying to build a spaceship, but I don't think girls are good at Legos."

I sit down on the floor. "I think girls, especially this one in particular," I dare a glance at Aislinn, pleased that her expression has softened somewhat, "are good at anything they put their minds to."

But he shakes his head mournfully. "Not spaceships."

I make an effort to contain my chuckle, but it slips through the corners of my mouth anyway. "You think we can teach her?"

His face lights up at the suggestion. "We sure can. I'm a good teacher."

"And what about your sisters? This is a pretty big set, we can probably use some help."

They both appear surprised to be included. The older one on the couch gives a quick shake of her head and shrinks back into the couch, tugging her sweatshirt over the cast on her wrist. The younger girl whispers something into Aislinn's ear.

"Kara would love to help," Aislinn murmurs, sliding one of the Lego-filled plastic bags over to her side.

For the next hour, we divide and conquer. Danny and I work on the first three bags while Aislinn and Kara build the other two, combining sections as needed.

The children are quietly cooperative. They keep their voices low and don't fight with each other.

"You know," Aislinn offers, not glancing up from her part of the ship, "Mr. King played with spaceships when he was a kid."

I haven't built a Lego set from scratch since my grandparents were alive, but the methodical nature of it is soothing. Every piece, no matter how small, has a place and a purpose. The directions must be followed exactly and in order.

Danny eyes me curiously. "What do you play with now?"

Kara interrupts. "Adults don't play. That's why they're so mad all the time."

"Sh. Mr. King isn't mad, and he's playing." Danny shoots his sister an annoyed look before looking back at me.

"Maybe you can ask my dad to join us. Maybe if he sees you playing, he'll want to play too."

Out of the corner of my eye, I see Kara edging even closer to Aislinn. "Sure," I agree, despite knowing that their father, even if he manages to crawl out of the gutter Burke and I dumped him in, will probably never have the fine motor coordination to build Legos. Or the ability to make a fist. He will never hurt anyone, ever again.

It's not until the spaceship is built and the kids are settled in front of the TV in their pajamas, that Aislinn and I make our goodbyes. The unexpected *rap* at the door has me instantly on alert, despite knowing who it most certainly isn't.

Davina stands up. "It's just Juliana, I asked her to drop off a few things on her way home."

"Juliana?" Aislinn repeats her name like a question. "I thought she was assigned to the team covering Los Muertos communications."

At my surprised glance, Aislinn adds, "I used my time wisely. Another day and I would have had a name for you."

"There is no mole," I say. "And since Juliana knows what it's like to be a kid on the receiving end of our services, I approved her request to become involved."

The frown creasing Aislinn's brow is still there when Davina opens the door. Juliana doesn't come in, merely handing over a bag containing the necessary documents to Davina.

By the time we exchange a few last words with Davina and the mother and step into the hall, Juliana is nowhere to be seen. As we wait for the elevator, Aislinn regards me thoughtfully. "I'm going to be working more closely with Davina. Would you mind if I meet with Juliana, get her perspective?"

A chime sounds just before the arrival of an empty elevator car. "Her perspective?"

"She must have some thoughts as to what these kids are going through, and ideas to help them start their news lives off on the right footing." We step inside and I jab at the button for the lobby. "Have you ever asked Juliana about her experience with The Network? If there's a way for us to ease the strain on these kids?"

I blink at her. "We do that by getting them away from the assholes making their lives hell."

"I guess." She sounds reluctant. "I wonder if there's a way we can keep in contact. Make sure that their lives have truly improved. That their mother doesn't fall for the same kind of guy and that they're not—"

"I think you're overthinking things."

Aislinn rubs at her forehead, a soft laugh trickling through her lips. "Probably. But it can't hurt."

I shrug. "Knock yourself out."

Aislinn beams as the doors open and we walk outside to the sidewalk. "Great, thanks."

"Come on, I'll give you a ride," I say, once we're standing on the sidewalk. What I really want to do is bring Aislinn back to my place.

She scans the street for a moment then looks up at me strangely. "You know, maybe those kids are onto something."

I tilt my head to the side, not following her train of thought. "What?"

"Adults think too much and don't play enough. Maybe that's why we're so cranky."

I frown. "I'm not cranky."

"Do you prefer curmudgeonly?"

"Possibly," I shoot back.

The corners of Aislinn's mouth edge upward into a wistful smile that makes my chest ache. "Good night, Damon. I'm going to walk."

"It's late, and Finley's place is twenty blocks away."

She turns around. "Twenty-six. But I'm tired of hiding behind tinted glass."

I exhale a deep sigh and jog until I catch up with her. "I'll walk you."

"It's a free country," she responds.

"Freedom is an illusion."

"Isn't that what you said about privacy?"

"That, too."

"Do you enjoy it?"

"Enjoy what?"

"The life you've created. Smoke and mirrors. Security cameras and tinted glass. Secrets and lies."

I scratch at my jaw. "I don't understand the question."

Aislinn stops in the middle of the sidewalk. "Are you happy, Damon?"

"Happiness is—"

"An illusion? Overrated?"

"No, I was going to say that happiness is elusive. Am I happy that those kids have a shot at a good life? Yes, that makes me happy."

"Did I—" She breaks off, turning away. "Forget it."

But I can't forget it. And I sure as fuck can't forget her. I wrap my hand around the silken curve of Aislinn's neck, my wrist disappearing within a glossy blonde waterfall. "Yes, you did. You do. Happy and miserable and angry and scared and hopeful and …" I tear my eyes away from Aislinn's glorious face to look at the sky for a long moment in an attempt to find clarity. When I have it, I look back down at my wife, my voice a gritted rumble. "Everything, Aislinn. You make me everything."

chapter forty-six

Aislinn

You make me everything.

What do I say to that?

Not a clue. I want to drop my panties, jump into Damon's arms, and offer him my body in return for those words.

You make me everything.

I'm so taken aback, so bewildered by what those four little words actually mean—by what I want them to mean—that I just start walking again.

Is it the same as "I love you"?

No. It's better.

One block passes in silence, then another. The tall high-rises of Midtown give way to the shorter, mostly older buildings of Finley's neighborhood. There is silence between us, but the noises of the city are a soundtrack all their own. Wheels on asphalt, the hum of music from open doors, the wail of sirens, pedestrians walking and talking, hailing cabs, swearing at cab drivers.

New York is a movie set with the camera constantly rolling. Are Damon and I just bit players in each other's lives? Because if we're meant to be together … shouldn't I know what to say right now? If this were a rom-com, shouldn't this be the part where our problems evaporate in the night mist? Love conquers all and we live happily ever after.

Right?

Clearly, someone needs to fire the director.

We arrive at Finley's apartment building. "Here we are," I mumble.

"What are you doing tomorrow?"

Damon's question is a surprise. "I'm meeting a realtor to look at apartments."

His brows pull together over the bridge of his nose. "You and Finley aren't getting along?"

"No, we are." I pause. "You knew we were sisters, didn't you?"

"Yeah." He nods. "Figured it was her truth to tell."

I can't fault him for that. Finley's prickly, and I'm glad she told me the truth herself. "I don't think she's your mole."

"There is no mole," he shoots back.

I decide not to argue. It's not as if I have proof to the contrary. "Anyway," I say, changing the subject, "it's time I get back to normal. A new normal. I'd like to feel settled before I start working with Davina. I've had enough of politics."

His deep chuckle sends a rush of goose bumps down my spine. "I don't blame you."

"What about you? Now that I'm not your problem anymore, have things gotten back to normal for you?"

His expression hardens. "Yeah. Guess they have."

The air between us becomes heavy. "Thanks for walking me back." I start to turn away before changing my mind. "That laptop I was using to research your employees—do you still have it?"

"Of course. It's in my office. Why?"

Because I never finished my work. "Because it probably has the appropriate security firewalls I need to take care of The Network business. Would you mind if I swing by to pick it up tomorrow?"

"No need, I'll bring it to you."

I push my hair behind my ear and allow myself a relieved smile. "Thanks."

"We'll do dinner. Drinks."

I cough. "Are you asking me on a date?"

He shrugs defensively. "Maybe."

"You don't date, remember?" I throw Damon's own words at him. "*One, I don't date. And two, I'm the filthiest motherfucker you'll ever meet.*"

His lips twist into that darkly seductive smirk that sends a rush of heat between my thighs. "Two is true enough. But as for one, you are the exception. For you, princess, I'd do anything."

chapter forty-seven

Damon

I've come a long way since my sloppy efforts to incriminate my stepfather backfired on me. I've learned that often, less is more. A few keystrokes. A wire transfer from a known criminal syndicate. And presto—a dickhead cop becomes a dirty cop.

This morning's headline proves it. **Dirty Cop Latest Victim of Gang Violence**

The investigation into the circumstances surrounding his death will be quietly abandoned. And there will be no elaborate hero's funeral for an officer who tarnished his uniform, no cameras pointed at the faces of his widow and children.

They are safe now.

And they are gone. Passengers on a pre-dawn flight to the destination of their choice.

I've come a long way, but in many ways, I'm not very different at all. I'm still that scared kid who's lived through the deaths of everyone who has ever mattered to him. My grandparents, my mother, Ace. Sure, I'm close to Finley and

Burke. And I'd take a bullet for anyone on my team. But there's a difference between letting someone into your life and giving them a piece of your soul.

I don't know whether I gave it to Aislinn or she took it—but a piece of me belongs to her all the same. That spitfire stole a piece of my heart.

And I haven't been whole since she left.

Did I evade the question that was really on her mind yesterday? Was "*You make me everything*" too vague? It's true … but is it enough?

I could have been more specific. I could have said *I love you*. That would be the truth too.

I don't know how I know, since I've only witnessed the romantic kind in the most unromantic of ways. The love between my mother and stepfather was sick and twisted. The love between Ace and Aislinn's mother was sad and unfulfilling. And I'm sure my grandparents loved each other, but my memory of them is faded and brittle.

Love. Such a simple, complicated word. A cliché.

It's instinctive, though. And it's true.

I love her.

I want Aislinn back because I'm in love with her. I need her back because living without her is untenable.

But I don't know how to address our last, heated exchange at my apartment. I don't know how to explain my epic failure to make Aislinn feel, not just safe, but *safe with me*.

Most importantly, I don't know how to fix it. Getting in touch with my emotions has never been high on my priority list, and it makes understanding Aislinn's actions and reactions—which do not seem to follow any linear string of logic I can pinpoint—damn near impossible.

However, I've beat impossible odds before. And yesterday, watching Aislinn playing with the kids, seeing the way they opened up to us, gave me an idea.

Today, Aislinn and I are going to play. I'll observe her strategy, get inside her head. Understand her.

There will be no crankiness involved at all. I've rented the VIP Room of a bar in the meatpacking district that is known as a millennial playroom of sorts. Full bar, pool tables, foosball, board games, and a DJ at night.

I am going to win Aislinn over.

While kicking her ass at Monopoly. And Jenga.

My mind drifts back to Aislinn's ass as I remember to grab the laptop she requested. Fuck, I miss the feel of her nestled against me during the night. The fullness that just exceeded my hands when I bent her over my lap. The smooth curves that look so damn good from every imaginable angle.

I open the desk drawer I'd shoved it in last week, but it's not there. Nor is it in any of the other drawers in my desk. Or my closet.

"Finley," I call as I walk out of my office. "Aislinn's laptop—have you seen it?"

Wholly engrossed in a spreadsheet on her screen, she glances up with a blank look. "Hmm?"

"Aislinn's laptop," I repeat.

"What about it?"

"Have you seen it?"

"It's not still in the office upstairs?"

I'd forgotten about the workstation Finley had set up for her there. A few minutes later, I'm staring at an empty docking station. No laptop.

I rub at my ears, trying to think through the buzzing. If I'd linked it with our in-house network, I could trace its location. But, since Aislinn specifically requested to stay off the grid, I have no way to ping its location.

I'm sure it will turn up somewhere. I buy computers by the dozen, and every one of my employees uses more than one. It's probably a simple mix-up.

The flash of my watch catches my eye as I run a hand through my hair.

Shit. I'm going to be late.

I arrive at Finley's apartment building to find Aislinn already waiting downstairs for me. I'm not sure whether to take it as consideration, or an unwillingness to invite me into Finley's apartment. She's wearing a sexy black jumpsuit, which hugs her curves in all the right places, but is just about the most inconvenient article of clothing ever invented.

An enticing challenge.

Her eyes drop to my empty hands. "You forgot the laptop, huh."

I feign contrition. "Shit, sorry."

"It's fine. I can have Finley bring it to me later."

To prevent her from texting or calling Finley immediately, I outstretch my arm and wriggle my fingers. Aislinn entwines hers with mine, our palms pressing together. I lead her to the car I've parked out front and open the passenger door. "No chauffeur-driven Navigator?" she asks, surprise threaded through her words.

"No tinted windows," I point out.

I bought the damn thing this morning.

Once we're both inside, I shift into gear and breathe in the new car smell mixed with Aislinn's particular honeyed scent. I don't drive myself often and I don't remember the last time a woman other than Finley was in the passenger seat. But I'd like to get used to it. At a red light, I move my hand to Aislinn's thigh, swiping my thumb over her knee.

Damn jumpsuit.

Hopefully next time it will be her bare skin that meets my touch.

"No bodyguards today?"

"They're around, but not too close." I gave specific orders

for my crew to be as discreet as possible.

"So, what's the plan?"

"I'll be building hotels on the Boardwalk and Park Place. You can slum it over on Baltic or Marvin Gardens."

"Monopoly? We're playing Monopoly?"

I give a grunt of acknowledgment. "Think you can manage not to go bankrupt for at least an hour?"

She narrows her eyes at me. "I don't trust you to be the banker."

"You don't trust me to handle Monopoly money?" I pretend to be offended. "Why not? I'm damn good with real money."

"Exactly. Which is why I'll be the banker."

"And how do I know you won't cheat?"

She dips her chin and raises her eyebrows simultaneously. I glance over at her and laugh. "Okay, you get to be Banker. But I get first choice of tokens."

She nods. "Let me guess, Battleship?"

"Of course. And you?"

"Well, I always went for the dog but I'm thinking I'll pick a different token today."

My stomach dips as I steer the car to the curb. "Good choice."

I slip my hand around Aislinn's waist and propel her through the door of the bar ahead of me. It's the kind of trendy hotspot I would never set foot in, which is precisely why I've chosen it for tonight. It's still early and instead of a DJ, instrumental music is piped through the speakers, bouncing off the exposed brick walls and low ceilings. The place feels like a cave. A cave with an enormous bar running the length of one wall and well-dressed twenty-somethings sprawled on leather furniture, playing classic board games while knocking back craft cocktails.

A guy in ripped jeans and a pretentious newsboy cap takes

one look at me and brings us to the private—well, semi-private since there's not an actual door—room I've reserved.

We order drinks and sit down at a chipped wooden table, the Monopoly board already arranged as I requested earlier. Aislinn's eyes are bright when they meet mine. "This is fun."

I grin in return. "That's the idea."

chapter forty eight

Aislinn

I've discovered something new about Damon.

He gloats. Oh, how he gloats.

He won at Monopoly. He won at Jenga.

And he almost won at Scrabble.

Almost.

Finally, after three hours of playing and losing, it is my turn to gloat.

Seeing how seriously Damon was taking the games, I had been drinking club soda. But with my win, I order champagne.

And that's when I learned something else about Damon. He's a terrible loser. "Are you recalculating my score?"

He looks up from the notepad with a frown stretched across his face. "I'm verifying."

"Maybe I should *verify* some of your words? I mean, what exactly is a qanat?"

"Go right ahead." He pushes the well-thumbed book across the table toward me. "But I can save you the trouble. It's an ancient type of tunnel, as well as an irrigation technique using the slope of the land."

I cross my arms over my chest and sigh. Of course, Damon would have an encyclopedic knowledge of underground exploration. He probably read the dictionary cover to cover too, judging by his word choices. *AGEE. MAGLEV. JIMPLY.*

I won with *MUTINY.*

I start pulling tiles from the crossword we've built on the game board and spell two words, from right to left and upside down, so that they face Damon.

HOW IRONIC.

He repeats them, then looks up at me with an expression that is both confused and mildly annoyed. "What are you trying to say?"

I tap the board with a fingernail.

"Why do you think I left?"

"You told me why. Because I asked you to replace Chad."

I bite the inside of my cheek. "So ... it was an act of defiance on my part. My way of rebelling against your authority?"

"Wasn't it?"

"No. I walked away from you because I am not a pawn on your chessboard any more than I am a stepping stone on the path of my father's ambitions."

"I asked. You said no. And that was the end of it."

"I understand our reasons for getting married weren't particularly romantic. But I still hoped ..." I take a moment to gather my thoughts. "I hoped my wins would be your wins, and your wins would be my wins."

Damon leans forward, his stare burning into me. "They're not?"

"No. I'm not sure we're playing the same game."

He doesn't argue with me. He doesn't say anything at all. In fact, Damon stands up and walks into the main part of the bar. A minute stretches into three. I sip at my champagne. *Would Damon leave me here?*

When my glass is empty and Damon still hasn't returned, I stand up and gather the jacket he left behind.

Just as I'm about to leave, Damon reappears wearing a triumphant smile. He takes his jacket from my hands and returns it to the back of the chair. "I've figured out the problem, come on."

"What—"

He cinches an arm around my waist and brings me into a larger room at the back of the space. He points at a chalkboard on the wall, our names scrawled at the bottom.

Aislinn + Damon.

My stomach clenches at the sight, happy and sad at the same time. There is another couple waving at us, standing behind a strip of tape glued to the floor. I look at Damon in confusion. "Darts?"

"You're right. We haven't been playing on the same team, and that stops now. Tonight it's darts, and tomorrow it's life." He takes my hand and drops something into it. No, not something. Tiles. Scrabble tiles, four of them. "Tonight. Tomorrow. The day after that. And the day after that."

I tear my eyes away from Damon's burning stare and glance at the tiles in my hand, easily configuring them into a word. *L O V E.*

My heart shudders inside my chest. But seeing the letters isn't enough. I need to hear Damon say the word. I keep my face impassive as I look at him. "Vole?"

The corners of his lips kick up. "Very funny. I'll unscramble it for you—after we win. It'll be your reward."

I roll my eyes and accept a set of darts. But inside, all I can think is, I already have my reward.

My savior. My savage. My devil. My dark knight.

And his name is Damon King.

chapter forty-nine

Damon

For a genius, I can be painfully obtuse.

Aislinn is a trophy worth fighting for.

But she is not a prize to be won.

Her love is meant to be earned.

I remind myself of that as I watch her take aim at the bull's-eye.

We are tied with Jack and Emma, who are surprisingly good. But when the dart flies from Aislinn's graceful fingers, it sails through the air to hit the board, dead-center. She turns to me with a huge grin on her face. "I'll take my reward now."

I lift her into my arms so that she's pressed against my chest, our faces even. I'm looking straight into the deep blue ocean of her eyes when I say, "Aislinn Granville King, I fucking love you. I've loved you since you were a Polaroid taped to a cement wall. I've loved you since you were a college kid volunteering at a women's shelter in a shitty neighborhood. I've loved you since you threw a shoe at my head, lit fire to my bed, and demanded that I kiss you."

Nerves clamor beneath my skin as I exhale an uncertain breath. "I don't know what it's like not to love you, princess." I am feared by criminals with no conscience. Respected by international power brokers with more wealth at their disposal than most countries. I've claimed victory over certain death more times than I can count.

But at this moment, all I need is to be loved by the woman I love. Desired by the woman I desire.

"Your smile is the light I want to live by, and your body is a treasure I would die for. The empire I've built means nothing without you by my side."

Aislinn hesitates, and I worry that I'm too late. That the kaleidoscope of emotions swirling on her face will ultimately end in rejection. That love—my love—will not be enough. Not nearly enough.

She regards me seriously. "I won't be an accessory, Damon. If you want me to sit beside you, your empire will look different than it does now. There will be no more business as usual."

"Good," I agree. "The only thing I care about is The Network. Everything else, everyone else—we can change, together."

She blinks several times, her lips pursing. "Do you really mean that?"

"I do. Be my wife, Aislinn. My equal. My queen. For real this time. Forever." I shut my mouth before I am reduced to begging, though for this woman I would crawl on my hands and knees through hot coals, begging all the way.

A single tear streaks down the elegant curve of Aislinn's cheekbone, trembling just at the corner of her lips. I plant a soft kiss there, licking at the salty droplet. And when I pull back, pure emotion shines from Aislinn's face. Not just any emotion.

Love.

But she says it anyway. "I love you, Damon. Even when I hated you. Even when I thought you were a bully, a devil, a savage. I cursed you and now I love you. So much."

Our mouths crash into each other, and out of the corner of my eye, I see Jack and Emma finally give up on congratulating us and walk away. Our kiss is an answer and a promise. It is an oath and a pledge.

We are partners in love and life.

Husband and wife.

I groan into her mouth. "Come home with me."

She rests her forehead against mine. "You are my home."

chapter fifty

Aislinn

Once Damon finally loosens his hold and I slide down the hard plane of his body, trembling from lust and love, he pulls my ring from his pocket and slides it onto my finger.

I'm never taking it off again.

"Come on." He slides his arm around my waist. "Let's get out of here."

I tuck the tiles into the zippered interior compartment of my purse, making a mental note to send a new Scrabble game here tomorrow. Because I am keeping these letters. Forever.

"I should text Finley, tell her I won't be coming back to her apartment tonight," I say, pulling out my phone once I'm back in Damon's car.

"Or ever," he adds, starting the engine and pulling away from the curb.

I bite down on a smile as I tap out a message to Finley.

Me: Sorted things out with Damon. Don't wait up for me. ;) xo

Her response is almost immediate.

Finley: Are you near my apartment? I left some paperwork on the kitchen table—would u mind grabbing it for me?

I glance over at Damon. "Any chance you can make a pit stop right now?"

"Any chance you can sit on my face later?"

My cheeks heat as I squirm in my seat. "Uh, sure." I swallow heavily as I look back at my phone. "That can definitely be arranged."

Me: No problem. On way now.

Damon pulls up in front of Finley's apartment and I jump out, feeling the burn of his stare on my back as I cross the sidewalk and enter the lobby.

I'm halfway to the kitchen when I hear a footstep behind me. I spin around, but just as I do, something connects with the side of my head. An explosion of pain at my temple becomes an avalanche, pulling me under.

I fight against it, coming to as I'm dragged along the floor, my hands tied at my back, my shoulder screaming. My vision is hazy, but there's no mistaking the familiar face of the woman doing the dragging.

Juliana.

"What are you doing? Get off me!" I yell.

She barely spares me a glance. "Shut up," she hisses.

"Damn it, you didn't hit her hard enough."

My head swivels in the other direction. *No. It can't be.*

But it is.

Chad grabs my other arm, yanking me upright. "You just couldn't leave well enough alone, could you? Juliana is so damn close to getting access to King's billions—and you would have ruined all of it."

"But, why?" I turn to Juliana. "Damon saved you. The

N—"

"The Network is bullshit. King got rid of my father. But it never occurred to him that my mother was just as bad. Just as violent as my dad when she was drunk, which was every day after we left. We had no family nearby anymore, no one who cared enough about us to notice what was going on or wonder why I wore long sleeves even in summer. King just made things worse."

chapter fifty-one

Damon

I hate letting Aislinn go. Not just because of my impatience to have her all to myself.

But because of the situation I'm allowing her to walk into.

Our conversation over Scrabble had me wondering who else on my team might disagree with the rules of my game. *Mutiny.*

I'd assumed Juliana's experience with The Network was entirely positive. But maybe it wasn't.

When I left Aislinn to add our names to the dartboard, I also talked through my suspicions with Finley. She agreed to "confide" in Juliana that Aislinn has been on the hunt for a mole in my organization and asked her to come back to the apartment to talk privately.

Finley would let Juliana know she wouldn't be leaving the office for several hours, and come up with a bullshit excuse to get Aislinn back to her apartment.

If I was wrong about Juliana, nothing would happen.

But if I was right, Juliana would want to plead her case to Aislinn.

I pull out my phone the minute the door closes, and log into Finley's security system. I am out of my car by the time Juliana appears on my screen.

White hot rage floods my veins when I see her lift something—a vase, maybe—and bring it down over Aislinn's head.

But that rage turns to terror when Lytton makes an appearance. What. The. Fuck?

I'd taken Sebastián Cruz's word that Lytton had disappeared, scared off when he heard about what I'd done to Michael. As I bound up the stairs, I'm cursing my carelessness at telling Burke and my guys to stand back.

Finley's front door flies open from the impact of my shoulder and I skid to a stop just as Lytton wraps an arm around Aislinn's neck, his other hand gripping a knife pointed at her jugular.

Time slows instantly, my vision tunneling to the three people less than twenty feet away from me and the drawn weapon that could have the love of my life bleeding out in front of me with a careless flick of the wrist. Aislinn is quiet, her eyelids fluttering.

My stance changes from offensive to defensive. I haven't drawn my gun, and my own knife is still tucked at my ankle. Slowly, I extend my arms, palms facing out so Lytton can see that they're empty. "Let go of my girl and you can walk out of here."

He shakes his head. "And walk straight into a trap? I don't think so."

"Fine. Tell me your endgame. As long as it includes Aislinn alive and unharmed, it's yours."

"My endgame was—*is*—your money, King. Make that happen and we've got a deal."

My eyes shift to Juliana. "What about you? What do you want out of this?"

She glances at Lytton, taking a tiny step away from him. "I just wanted to shut down The Network, to change the way you do things."

"So you teamed up with this asshole?"

At Juliana's wince, I have my answer. Lytton played her and she fell for him.

"Fuck off," Lytton spits. "I was going to take your place. Become the conduit between politicians and crime bosses. It took some pressure, but—"

"By pressure, you mean exposing his money launderer?"

"Yes. And we couldn't just get rid of you, not without getting access to your crypto-cash first."

"It wasn't about the money," Juliana yells, taking another step to the side.

Lytton flashes her an exasperated look. "It's always about the goddamn money."

"Fine. Put down the knife and I'll give you whatever you want." Not true, of course. Chad Lytton is as good as dead, but not until Aislinn is safe.

A fact of which he is well aware.

"No," he says, shaking his head. Aislinn winces as the knife digs into the flesh of her neck, a bright red drop rolling down her creamy skin. "You're not winning this one."

Burke and my team will be here any second. But they could easily make things worse. I need to end this now.

"Damon's a really sore loser," Aislinn manages to wheeze. "It's much better to be on his team." She lifts her knee and stomps her pointed heel into Lytton's shoe at the same time as she spins to the side.

I'm across the room before he's even gathered breath to yell, catching his wrist and using my forward momentum to turn the blade on him. "Checkmate, motherfucker." It plunges through the soft space between Lytton's collarbone like room-temperature butter.

I let him drop to the ground and sweep Aislinn into my arms, keeping an eye on Juliana who has backed her way into the corner, hands covering her mouth as tears stream from her eyes.

"You make a good teammate, princess. But I'm done playing—the stakes are too high."

epilogue

Aislinn
Two Months Later

*O*n our flight to the Seychelles, I made Damon promise to try my favorite drink of all time: the piña colada.

We arrived a few hours ago, were escorted to our private villa, and wasted no time ordering drinks and slipping into our private plunge pool. "Try it," I say, tapping the husk of my pineapple against the husk of Damon's, then biting my lip to stifle a laugh as the tip of his umbrella pokes him in the eye.

He shoots me a wry look, yanking the offending embellishment from his drink and tossing it aside. "I thought I gave the staff specific instructions: the umbrellas are for my wife, only."

I set my drink down and maneuver myself to straddle Damon's lean hips, my naked breasts skimming his muscled torso with each inhale. "Yes. And your wife counteracted that order. Umbrellas for the happy couple."

He dips his fingers into the fruity concoction, scooping some out and dabbing a generous portion on my nipples. I gasp as they furl into needy peaks, though I don't pull away. When Damon's fingers trace the line of my clavicle and the pulsing hollow between, I am staring directly into his dark, burning gaze. "We are, aren't we?" There's an air of surprise in his rumbled baritone.

Not at us, exactly. His surprise is directed inward, aimed at that little boy still inside of him. The one who believed himself unworthy of happiness. The one who felt doomed to loss and heartbreak. To a life where joy came from the destruction of his enemies rather than shared triumphs with his allies.

And I am definitely Damon King's ally. His partner in life and love.

His princess and his queen.

His wife.

"Yes. We most certainly are," I agree, just before his mouth closes over one of my breasts, his teeth grazing the sensitive skin as my head falls back, the wet ringlets of my hair sliding down my back and into the clear blue water surrounding us.

Happiness is definitely in our grasp these days. It is a hard-won, precious thing. A state of being Damon and I have grabbed with relentless determination. And gratitude. As firmly and fiercely as we embrace each other right now.

Our journey has been rocky, to say the least. After that night in Finley's apartment, I wasn't at all sure we would be capable of finding a balance.

And I wasn't sure that love, even when I was holding those Scrabble tiles in my hands, would be enough. What we had was real—but would it be enough to carry us through the highest highs and the lowest lows? Could we find a mutually acceptable plateau, a place to be … happy?

Our honeymoon is a temporary respite from the barely controlled chaos of our lives in New York City, and a much-needed opportunity to rest and recharge.

When we return, in addition to my commitment to The Network, I will have a mayoral campaign to run, although it won't be my father's. He recently announced his intent to step down from office after his term, and that despite rumors to the contrary, his future plans do not include Gracie Mansion. I am throwing my support behind a candidate both Damon and I back wholeheartedly. Davina Richardson. She will win—not just because I am damn good at my job. But because she is the woman our city deserves. And I will make sure every eligible voter knows it.

My mother is still holding on. Slipping further and further into her own mind every day, but she seems happy there. Once or twice, when I've sat quietly at her side for long enough, she will even share stories of her and Ace. She's not actually talking to me, more like recounting her memories to herself. But the past, specifically her past with Ace, has become my mother's own happy place. I don't begrudge her that, at all.

Finley has become more like a sister every day. We bicker and drive each other batty, but she is my family now and I love her. More than that. I respect her. And thankfully, the feeling is entirely mutual.

Juliana ... Well, Damon and I weren't sure what to do about Juliana. Once I got him to see beyond his rage at Juliana's betrayal, he realized that her actions were an extension of the damage caused by domestic abuse. She agreed to check into an inpatient recovery center and I've visited her several times already and used her experiences to make The Network more supportive of families *after* we transition them into new lives.

Life is good. And it's about to get even better.

Damon pulls off my breast, swirls more of his cold drink around his mouth and licks his way up my neck with firm, cold strokes. Goose bumps prickle my flesh, chills racing down my spine. Neither of us are wearing bathing suits, and with a roll of my hips, Damon's cock is notched at my entrance. His hands wrap around my waist, pushing my body down through the buoyancy of the water.

"Like puzzle pieces," I say on a sigh, marveling at the perfect way we fit together.

"You gonna come apart on me?" he growls, his still cold tongue pushing between my lips.

I don't answer. I can't. Our kiss deepens, shards of my composure breaking loose as we begin moving against each other.

Besides, the answer is obvious. *Yes.* Yes, I'm going to come apart in Damon's arms. Just as I've done hundreds of times before. Not only will he be there to catch me, but his love will put me back together again. Every. Single. Time.

Damon

I'm just uncorking a bottle of champagne when Aislinn joins me on the terrace of our private villa. After our afternoon lounging in the pool, Aislinn took a nap while I went for a long run around the island. I also checked in with Finley, Burke, and even Sebastián. True to his word, he has pulled his father's men in line. Los Muertos is operating in New York again, not quite at full strength, but close. Tensions are simmering with the Albanians though, and the Korean street gangs are encroaching on territory dominated by the Trinitarios. Although I am across the globe, Manhattan is never far from my thoughts.

"I ordered dinner while you were in the shower," I say, motioning toward the table. Her hair is damp, a white sundress billowing around her lithe frame from the early evening breeze. "I thought we could eat out here."

A still sleepy smile pulls at Aislinn's mouth as she comes to my side. My arm instinctively curls around her waist, cinching her against me. She juts her chin toward the explosion of color streaking across the sky. "Did you order the sunset too? It's spectacular."

I press a kiss against her forehead. "You're spectacular."

And she is. Aislinn's sharp edges have softened since we first met, the crackling intensity of her fire turned down a notch. She still burns though, much like the inflamed horizon. The brightness of her light remaining, not only undimmed but expanding to include an infinite range of colors. This woman embodies an entire universe of beauty. Spectacular, indeed.

With my free hand, I pour champagne into two flutes. Before I can offer one to Aislinn, she says, "I think maybe I'll just have another daiquiri with dinner."

I don't bother to hide my grimace. "Not sure I'm impressed with the bartender here. I accidentally took a sip of yours earlier today and there couldn't have been a drop of rum in it."

The words aren't out of my mouth before the impact of them slams into my brain. One look at Aislinn's face is all the confirmation I need. There is joy and pride and … a hesitant uncertainty.

From the way her eyes have gone wide, scrutinizing my expression as intently as I am hers, Aislinn's nerves come not from the unknown, or the new life she's carrying—they are for me.

She angles her body toward mine, the heavy pink sun descending into an endless sea just over her bare shoulder, words tumbling from her glossy lips. "I only just found out. I wasn't sure how to tell you. So much has happened, we're just learning how to make a life together as a couple and now—"

"And now we will do exactly that, as a family." A wave of emotion comes over me and I drop to my knees before this woman who swept into my life like a storm. Lightning and thunder, violent winds and drenching rain, but most of all, the brightest of suns. She exposed my roots, rocked my stability. All for the better.

And now, there is more change to come. More of Aislinn. More of us.

I welcome it. All of it. All of her.

All of us.

I drag my face over the still flat slope of Aislinn's belly, breathing in the scents of honey and sunshine and the pungent sweetness intrinsic to this woman alone. "Are you okay with all this? It's a lot, I know. I think it happened that first night I came back. I started a new prescription when I came back but there was a gap of those days that I was away. It completely slipped my mind that …"

I have a very low threshold for mistakes. But this one feels like a gift. The greatest gift, second only to Aislinn herself.

I swallow past the tightness of my throat, so overwhelmed with gratitude that I can barely push out two words. "Thank you."

Thank you for being the light to my dark.
Thank you for being the queen to my king.
Thank you for everything.

The End

I hope you loved
Aislinn and Damon's story!

Can't get enough of Damon and Aislinn?
I have an extended epilogue just for you—meet
baby King!
http://smarturl.it/WagesBonus

Read on for a sample of
Throne of Lies!

chapter one
November 2007

Jolie

"I can't believe you and Daddy are making me do this."

"Jolie, I don't understand your attitude. This is a privilege, not a punishment." There was a flush on Nina's cheeks that I'd only seen after I came home from school, usually while she was sipping a glass of Rosé. But it wasn't even noon yet, and the patches on her cheeks were from annoyance rather than alcohol. "Do you even know what an honor it is to be chosen? This tradition dates back years."

I stifled a yawn as Nina launched into yet another history lesson on the origins of the International Debutante Ball. By now I could repeat it, verbatim, in my sleep. Normally, I liked my stepmother, I really did. My own mother died before I was in kindergarten, and Nina was a vast improvement over the revolving door of paid employees that had raised me until a few years ago, when Nina moved in and never left. She was only fifteen years older than me and felt more like an older sister than a stepmother. While that may have bothered others, I enjoyed having someone young and fun to hang around with.

Finally, I interrupted. "You could have at least let me choose my own date. I haven't seen Remington Montgomery in years—I barely even remember him." I knew I was blaming Nina unfairly, but this entire affair had rubbed me the wrong way. First of all, it was absolutely galling that debutantes didn't have dates, they had 'escorts'—like we needed someone with a penis to shepherd us through this overhyped snob-fest. And then for my father to insist my *escort* be the son of his business partner . . . it made me want to scream.

Not that I had anything against Remington. How could I? We'd only met a handful of times, despite living just a few blocks from each other on Manhattan's Upper East Side our entire lives. But he was a couple of years older than me, maybe three, and we'd always gone to different schools.

"He seems like a lovely boy," Nina said, her tone measured and clearly intending to soothe, but maddening all the same.

"Well, I hope you recognize him, because I don't know that I will."

Nina plucked a nonexistent piece of lint from her dress, lips twitching from holding back a bemused smile. "I'm sure everything will work out just fine. Today is only a brunch, Jolie. Maybe I'll sneak you a Mimosa to get you to relax."

I sent my eyes skyward, a gesture that seemed the most appropriate response to just about anything Nina or my father said these days. "Is that a promise?"

When Nina didn't answer, I sighed and looked out the window. The actual Debutante Ball was still a month away, but today was one of the pre-ball activities. It wasn't called a season for nothing. Besides the Bachelor Brunch, there was the Mother-Daughter Luncheon, Father-Daughter

Luncheon, Pre-Ball Cocktail Party, and Post-Ball Reception.

Yes, it really was called the Bachelor Brunch. And no, we weren't contestants in a reality show. Although by this point, it wouldn't have surprised me to come out of this experience with a dowry and a betrothal—or at least a red rose.

Remington Montgomery. The last time I saw him was at some award ceremony a few years ago, honoring our fathers. He'd been tall, that I remembered, mostly because I had a habit of scouring every room for people my height or taller. At seventeen, most boys my age were finally catching up with me, although I said a prayer every night that I would stop growing. I was five-eight and a half, and wanted to keep it that way . . . except my favorite pair of jeans hinted that I'd recently climbed closer to five-nine.

Anyway, that was all I could remember about Remington. He was tall. Or at least, he'd appeared tall back then. Brown hair or blond, surfer-boy cute or gamer-geeky—I hadn't a clue.

"Will you recognize him?" I prodded Nina, my voice climbing higher from nerves.

"Hmmm?" Nina had been staring out the window, too. It probably would have been quicker to walk from our apartment than to take a car, but even I wouldn't want to walk twenty-blocks in the shoes I'd squeezed into. I could have sworn they fit a month ago when Nina dragged me to Bergdorfs.

"Remington. Will you recognize him?"

"Of course. At least, I think so. But don't worry. Your father will be there, and I'm sure Remington's—"

"Why didn't Daddy come with us from home?"

"Honey, you know your father has to work."

"But it's Saturday. And he wanted me to do the whole debutante thing as badly as you did. The least he could do is suffer along with me," I grumbled, despite being well aware that my father worked all the time, and weekends were no exception.

As the car finally glided to a stop at the curb, Nina reached out to give my hand a reassuring squeeze. "For now, you've got me. Think you can make do?"

I relented. Even if my father had been sitting beside me, his face would probably be buried in the *Wall Street Journal* or an industry research report. I should be grateful Nina was by my side. "Sorry, I really don't mean to be such a brat. Thanks for being here."

My stepmother's pretty face brightened as her lips pulled into a smile. "You're not a brat, Jolie. You're a debutante."

The ridiculousness of the statement sent a matching grin onto my face. "Not sure if that's a promotion, but I'll take it." I followed her out of the car, keeping my knees together to avoid flashing the waiting society page photographers—I wasn't wearing a floor length white gown just yet.

This year's Bachelor Brunch was being held at an elegant French restaurant. Nina and I walked beneath a white canopy and through the double doors held open by men wearing dark suits and earpieces. Security was to be expected. The last name of every debutante could be found somewhere on the Forbes 400. Inside, the lights were soft, every available surface sporting floral arrangements with this year's colors—pink and gold.

It smelled like a greenhouse, and felt just as humid.

Just beyond the lobby entrance, people weren't mingling so much as clumping together by age and gender. Groups of teenaged girls looked around like frightened rabbits, eyes jumping between their parents and their escorts-to-be. Young men sporting fraternity ties shifted nervously from foot to foot, looking like they wished they were holding lacrosse sticks instead of sodas. Wealthy magnates, clutching crystal tumblers filled with liquor, crowed about their latest hostile takeover or international negotiation while their middle-aged society wives showed off their latest *Guilt Gift*, designed to distract them from their husband's most recent affair.

"I think I see Lily Montgomery, but I'm not sure which of those boys is her son," Nina said, sticking close to me. Reluctance to shoulder her way in with what appeared to be a primarily First-Wives Club came off her in waves.

Spotting a small group of women who resembled Nina at the back of the room—early thirties, blonde, fit, and wearing trendy clothes designed to show off their figures rather than hide their flaws—I tipped my chin in their direction.

"Ah, my tribe." Her grateful grin faded as she turned back to me. "I don't see your father yet and to be honest, all these boys look the same to me. Will you be okay?"

I squared my shoulders, feeling better now that I knew we were both in the same leaky boat. "I'll be fine. Promise."

She rested a perfectly manicured hand on my shoulder. "Your father will be here soon, I'm sure of it."

I nodded, even knowing it was an empty promise. With my dad, work always came first. But at least Nina and I had each other, and I could surely survive the next few hours without drowning myself in a punchbowl. "I know. Now stop hovering. I'll be fine."

Nina stepped back, and I watched her weave through the round tables marked by elegant numbered placards and adorned with extravagant pink and gold centerpieces. Hoping to avoid introducing myself to a bunch of strangers all at once, I turned back toward the entrance on the chance of linking up with a straggler instead.

The front door opened, a lone figure propelled forward on a burst of blinding sunlight. Once it receded, my gaze landed on a pair of calm gray eyes, half-hidden by a tuft of hair the color of the roan pony I'd ridden as a child, the ends curling over the collar of his navy blazer.

A frisson of recognition shot through me at the exact instant an unfamiliar ache warmed me to my bones. Remington Montgomery. He looked nothing like the boy I only vaguely remembered, but I knew it was him all the same.

One look cast an invisible tether between us, a lure that hooked over my collarbone with an almost audible *clank* and entirely eliminated my reluctance to be here. Needing to ease the sudden, sharp pain inside my chest, I instinctively took a few steps forward.

The door opened again. Another beam of sunlight streaked inside, this time revealing my father and his business partner, Remington's father. Stepping into the lobby, they flanked him, both clapping opposite shoulders. Remington didn't wince, his eyes widening just enough to convey his restraint at not shrugging them both off. "I see you've already found each other," my dad said, looking between us as he commented on the obvious.

I nodded, not trusting my voice quite yet.

Remington answered with a curt but respectful, "Yes, sir." Once our fathers had strolled off in search of a drink or a potential client, probably both, he finally addressed me. "I almost didn't recognize you. You've gotten—"

"Taller," I interrupted, ducking my head.

He closed the remaining distance between us with a rolling stride, waiting until I'd raised my head again before correcting me. "Actually, I was going to say prettier."

At six-three, or maybe six-four, Remington towered over me, and I had to tilt my head back to meet his eyes. Long lashes cast shadows atop high cheekbones that slid sharply to his lips. Full and almost pretty, they were the perfect accent to soften his hard, patrician features.

A flush broke over my skin, a sudden warmth throbbing between my thighs. The first tender stirrings of lust swirling inside my otherwise empty stomach.

"Thanks, Remington," I forced out through paralyzed vocal chords.

"My name's kind of a mouthful. Just call me Tripp, everyone else does."

Tripp. I hadn't realized he went by a nickname, but it suited him. "I take it you're a 'third'?"

"Unfortunately for me, yes." He pushed that same errant tuft of hair back again and glanced over my shoulder, his face showing a trace of resignation as he took in the crowd I'd retreated from just a few minutes before, forcing a sideways smile onto his lips. "Can I be honest with you?"

Uh oh. Nothing good starts with that question. I squared my shoulders, bracing myself. "Sure."

"I wasn't looking forward to this."

That made two of us. "Ditto."

He turned surprised eyes back to me. They were an interesting shade of gray, like the sliver of horizon suspended between the sea and sky on an overcast day. A place you could try swimming toward but never reach. "I thought all girls were into these kinds of things."

A blush burned my cheeks, and I curled my fingers into my palms, indenting my flesh with the half-moon shape of my nails. "Not this girl."

"How long do you think we have to stay?"

Except that suddenly I wasn't very keen on leaving. "Um . . . I'm not sure. Maybe a couple of hours."

Mischief turned his gray stare silver. "How about we give it our all for the next hour and then get out of here?"

"If you want to go, I'm sure it's fine. I don't want to keep you here or anything," I stammered, fighting to keep the sharp sting of disappointment from my tone.

His brows, two shades darker than the hair on his head, pulled together. "You're coming with me, of course."

"Oh." It was just a soft puff of air as Tripp pressed his hand against the flat of my back and led me into the main dining room.

You're coming with me.

Did Tripp feel what I was feeling? Even one-tenth of what I was feeling? One-hundredth? The current that seemed to run between our bodies, energy sparking at the slightest touch, a magnetic pull tugging us together—he had to be feeling it, too. Right?

Of course.

If you enjoyed this peek of THRONE OF LIES it's available now!
http://smarturl.it/TOLAmzn

more from tara leigh

The Wages of Sin Duet
Cruel Sanctuary
Corrupt Savior

The Lies Duet
Throne of Lies
Legacy of Lies

Nothing But Trouble
Rock King
Rock Legend
Rock Rebel

Billionaire Bosses
Deal Breaker
Penthouse Player

about the author

Tara Leigh is a multi-published author of steamy contemporary romance. A former banker on Wall Street, she graduated from Washington University and holds an MBA from Columbia Business School, but she much prefers spending her days with fictional boyfriends than analyzing financial spreadsheets. Tara currently lives in Fairfield County, Connecticut with her husband, children, and fur-baby, Pixie.

let's keep in touch

Made in the USA
Lexington, KY
30 June 2019